SAMMY FERAL'S
Diaries of

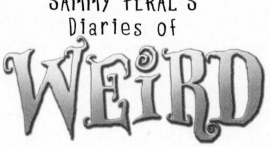

SAMMY FERAL'S
Diaries of
WEiRD

Eleanor Hawken
Illustrations by John Kelly

Quercus

Quercus

New York • London

Text © 2012 by Eleanor Hawken
Illustrations © 2012 by John Kelly

Any member of educational institutions wishing to photocopy part or
all of the work for classroom use or anthology should send inquires to
Permissions c/o Quercus Publishing Inc., 31 West 57th Street, 6th Floor,
New York, NY 10019, or to permissions@quercus.com.

ISBN 978-1-62365-032-2

Library of Congress Control Number: 2013937916

Distributed in the United States and Canada
by Random House Publisher Services
c/o Random House, 1745 Broadway
New York, NY 10019

Manufactured in the United States

2 4 6 8 10 9 7 5 3 1

www.quercus.com

For Caroline, Adam, and Charlotte—
my original feral family

Friday April 3rd

Hi, I'm Sammy Feral. I've never had a reason to keep a diary—until now. Today my world did a total 180. I've lost my family, narrowly escaped death, and discovered that werewolves are more than just a story made up to scare kids.

This diary is evidence to prove I'm not insane when the men in white coats try to wheel me away to the loony bin.

I'd better start from the beginning . . .

I live in a small town called Tyler's Rest. Nothing exciting ever happened here—until today. The most interesting thing about Tyler's Rest is Feral Zoo—it's won "Zoo of the Year" three times and is home to the world's oldest gorilla living in captivity.

My family owns Feral Zoo, and that makes me pretty popular.

This is my family . . .

DAD

Job: Owner of Feral Zoo

Looks like: Overtired ape in a suit

Age: Older than Mom but younger than Darwin, the oldest gorilla in Feral Zoo

Can be found: His office

Favorite animal: Cheetah cos he's always running around at top speed

MOM

Job: Chief zookeeper (both at home and at work)

Looks like: A lioness with frizzy golden hair

Age: BIG secret

Can be found: Breeding rare tigers and bugging me about school

Favorite animal: Llama (dumb creatures if you ask me)

GRACE

Job: Older sister and zoo-keeping apprentice

Looks like: Girly girl in a zookeeper's uniform

Age: 17

Can be found: Kissing her boyfriend Max behind the aviary at lunchtime

Favorite animal: Dolphin (Boring! Sharks are way cooler)

NATTY (SHORT FOR NATALIE)

Job: Little sister and most annoying person on planet Earth

Looks like: Hyperactive squirrel monkey

Age: 6

Can be found: Following me around and making more noise than a pack of hyenas at feeding time

Favorite animal: Hamster (Even more boring than a dolphin)

And this is what you should know about me . . .

SAMMY

Job: Helping out at Feral Zoo to earn pocket money

Looks like: Freckly face like a tree frog

Age: 12

Can be found: Cleaning out snake tanks, feeding crocodiles, and hanging out with my best friend, Mark

Top five animals (can't pick just one):

1   Pythons
2   Jumping spiders
3   Great white sharks
4   Wolves (until today)
5   Iguanas

So that's me and my family—and here's why our lives will never be the same again . . .

After school today I was helping out at the zoo as normal. I'd finished feeding the gorillas and was on my way to visit Khan, our mega-grouchy Sumatran tiger, when I stopped off at the reptile house to feed Beelzebub.

Beelzebub is my pet python. I helped him hatch as a baby and he lived in a tank in my bedroom for a year. But then he escaped and tried to eat Natty while she was sleeping, so now Mom makes me keep him at the zoo.

I got to the reptile house and pushed open the door with my shoulder (cos I was holding a box of Beelzebub's favorite frozen field mice). A strange-looking teenage boy was standing in the middle of the room. He smiled when I walked in, as if he'd been waiting for me to arrive.

There was no one else in there, so when the door slammed shut we were alone. I ignored him, thinking he was just another zoo visitor, and walked over to Beelzebub's vivarium. As I lowered the frozen mice into the tank I could feel the boy's eyes burning into the back of my head.

"Hey, Sammy," he said. "I'm Donny. I'm here to help you."

Er . . . minor freak-out!

How did he know my name without asking?

Was he psychic? Was he a crazy stalker? Or was he something else . . . ?

DONNY

Age: 17 (although he has gray hair like my granddad did)

Looks: As cool and calm as an alley cat

First impressions: This guy is seriously weird!

I figured that Donny was probably just a new zookeeper and that's how he knew who I was—everyone at Feral Zoo knows me.

I held out the box of frozen mice toward Donny, thinking he'd take one and feed it to a snake. But he just stood there.

I stared back.

That's when I noticed Donny didn't look like a zookeeper. He was wearing a plain white

8

T-shirt, ripped jeans, and motorcycle boots—not exactly regular zoo-keeping gear.

"How's Caliban?" Donny asked, bending down and studying a rare Peruvian boa constrictor winding around a damp log.

I should have explained earlier that Caliban is our new puppy. We've only had him three weeks. Caliban spends every day sitting in Dad's office. The man who sold him to Dad said he was a purebred husky. He was lying.

I shrugged my shoulders at Donny and ignored him while I fed Beelzebub a few more field mice. At the time I was more interested in the way Beelzebub dislocated his jaw to swallow the mice (such a cool trick—wish I could do it with burgers) than wondering how Donny knew about Caliban. Now I wish I'd paid more attention—maybe then I could have saved my family.

Donny walked over and tugged my arm.

"Look, if you're ever in trouble," he whispered, "or if things get really weird, just let me know. I love weird. Weird is totally up my street."

Er, excuse me? What? This guy was making no sense.

Then Donny stuffed something into my hand.

"Remember," he said, looking me right in the eye, "I can help." Then he just walked off, like nothing had happened.

I looked down at what Donny had slipped into my hand—it was a card.

This card:

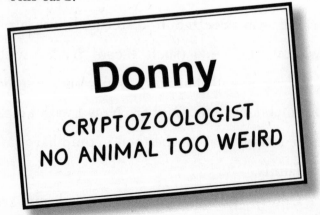

Donny

CRYPTOZOOLOGIST
NO ANIMAL TOO WEIRD

What's a cryptozoologist?

The word was like it was from an alien language—I had no idea what it meant.

So I did what I always do when I want to know something—I went to see Dad.

"What's a cryptozoologist?" I asked as we sat down for a snack in the zoo café.

"Someone who studies animals that don't exist," Dad said, biting into his ham sandwich. Dad knows the answer to everything. "Like the abominable snowman, or dragons, or werewolves."

Yep, that confirmed it—Donny was a weirdo of the highest degree. But why was he interested in me?

Anyway . . . the rest of the afternoon was pretty normal. Dad had a meeting with a panda breeder who was visiting from China. Grace trained a chimp to wave. Natty and Mom took turns throwing steaks into the tiger den, and I cleaned out the spider tanks. One of the black widows had eaten her mate—cool!

After all the visitors had left I headed toward Dad's office. The plan was to round everyone up and go home for dinner.

But things never, *ever* go according to plan.

It was dark outside and the light of a full moon illuminated the animal cages as I walked through the zoo. I could hear barking coming from Dad's office. It sounded like Caliban.

Caliban's growls got louder and louder as I opened the office door. "Caliban, chill . . ." I started, but I never finished my sentence.

I was way too freaked out by what I saw . . .

As the door swung back I could see Dad sitting behind his desk. Instead of tapping away at his computer, he was staring into space and drooling.

He had bite marks on his neck, huge ones—

it looked as if he'd been bitten by some kind of animal.

"Dad?" I chuckled nervously, hoping he was playing a game.

Dad didn't answer. He made a strange growling sound and curled his lips like an angry dog.

Huh?!

My brain scrambled to understand what was going on.

I took a step closer to Dad's desk, and stepped on something soft. I looked down and saw Natty's hand.

My eyes nearly popped out of my head in horror. Mom, Grace, and Natty were all lying on the office floor. All as still as stone.

I stopped feeling confused—I felt terrified. Everyone looked dead!

I didn't know whether to puke, laugh, or cry— it didn't seem real.

Behind the thumping sound of
my heart I could hear snarling
coming from the corner of
the room.
I looked
up and
saw Caliban
licking his lips.
He paced
toward
me slowly,
reminding
me of a hungry
wolf stalking its
prey. He looked

larger than I remembered and a whole lot more
terrifying.

"Caliban?" I gulped.

Caliban raised his eyes to the ceiling and let
out a mega-loud howl. The sound made my legs

turn to jelly and wobble beneath me.

I had no idea what was happening, but whatever it was I just wanted it to stop. But it didn't stop . . . It just got worse . . .

From the corner of my eye I saw Grace pick herself up off the floor. Only she didn't look like Grace—her teeth looked larger, her ears were poking upward from the top of her head, and her nose was twitching like mad.

Surely I must be dreaming? None of this could be happening.

Then thick fur started to sprout all over Dad's face . . .

Er, rewind! Face fur?? Yep—face fur!

My brain went into overdrive as I tried to understand what was happening. Was I going nuts? I blinked my eyes like a madman—hoping to wake up from a horrible dream. But I wasn't asleep.

I desperately looked over at Mom. Mom's

always great in a crisis—if anyone could make things right, it was her. But instead of helping me, Mom crouched down on all fours, and a tail—that's right, a tail—ripped through her trousers and started to grow out of the base of her back.

Sound crazy? It gets crazier . . .

Natty pulled herself onto her feet like a newborn zombie and let out a howl even louder than Caliban's. Then she dropped on to all fours and looked more like a dog than a six-year-old girl.

My sister was a dog??!!

Without thinking, I inched backward, ready to run.

Something leaped through the air toward me. Caliban.

There was a muddy shovel propped against the wall. I reached over and swung it through the air. It skimmed the end of Caliban's nose and he backed away from me.

I thought I'd scared him off. But no—I'd made him MAD!!

Caliban arched his back and growled viciously. He no longer looked like a friendly puppy—he looked like a deadly wolf! Mad rage filled his eyes as he dug his knife-sharp claws into the floor. He slowly put one paw in front of the other as he crept toward me.

I gulped and backed away, into a corner. My back slammed into the wall—there was nowhere else to go.

I desperately swung the shovel again, but a heavy blow hit my arm and made me drop it. It was wolf-Dad—he'd knocked the shovel clean out of my hands with a swipe of his tail!

This is it, I thought. I'm gonna die, right here, right now. There were five wolves and one of me. My chances of survival seemed as likely as a mongoose becoming a pop star.

There was nothing else I could use to defend myself—I was wolf meat, for sure. I stared into the eyes of the beasts that used to be my family and frantically tried to think of a plan . . . What could I do . . . ?

* Call the other zookeepers for help? They'd never get here in time!
* Phone Mark and shout SOS? There was no time for phone calls!
* Run away and not look back? How could I escape?
* Find someone who knew the first thing about people turning into wolves? Er . . . who?

I was out of ideas . . . I had nowhere to hide and no one to turn to. The wolves were inches away from me—I could feel the heat of their breath on my face, could hear the smack of their tongues licking their lips.

I closed my eyes and prepared to die . . .

But I didn't die. Instead Dad's office filled with the sound of howling wolves. After a few seconds I opened my eyes to see a teenage boy standing in the doorway. The moonlight was bouncing off his silver hair.

Donny!

He was firing darts from a silver blowpipe in his mouth. The darts were shooting at 100 mph— like Donny was a human machine gun.

I watched in shock as a dart struck one of Dad's paws. Dad's dog-like body fell to the ground. Then Donny shot them all, one by one. Mom, Grace, Natty, even Caliban—they didn't stand a chance! Soon all five of them were lying motionless on the floor.

First everyone turns into wolves, then they all get shot dead with blow darts?!

Freak-out supreme!

I felt beyond sick—it felt as if my stomach was living inside my throat!

Donny calmly put his blowpipe back in his pocket. "I told you to call me if things got weird," he said, smiling like nothing had happened. "Luckily for you I stuck around. Any spare cages in the zoo?" he asked, scanning the room.

My eyes darted from Donny to the bodies of the five wolves on Dad's office floor.

The inside of my mouth felt like a desert, and for a split second I forgot how to speak.

"Huh?" I finally managed to say. "You've killed them!" The words stuck in my mouth. "You've just killed my entire family!"

"Relax." Donny shrugged, as if I was overacting. "They're not dead, just sleeping. These are tranquilizer darts. We need to get them behind bars before they wake up. Can't have a bunch of werewolves wandering around a zoo, can we?"

"Werewolves?" I repeated like a dumb parrot. The word felt strange in my mouth—as if for the first time I understood what it *really* meant.

Werewolves . . . Are you kidding me? It was all way too bizarre to get my head around.

I watched Donny bend over Grace and inspect her sleeping wolf body. Then I remembered what Dad had said about cryptozoologists—they studied animals that didn't exist. Animals like werewolves. If Donny was right, and everyone had been turned into werewolves, then he was the only person that could help me.

Donny took hold of Grace's tail and dragged her across the floor.

"Wait a minute!" I shouted, holding up a hand. Watching him treat my sister like an animal was horrible.

Donny looked up at me with a raised eyebrow, like he couldn't understand what my problem was.

What *was* my problem? Was I freaking out about the werewolves? Was I freaking out about Donny being so calm—why wasn't he freaking out too?

My brain raced . . . I had a choice to make. I could let Donny help—even if it did involve silver darts and dragging Grace around by her tail—or I could go it alone. I didn't like my odds for dealing with werewolves alone. I might not be so lucky next time.

The conclusion: I *had* to let Donny help.

Donny was the only thing standing between me and werewolf attack!

"It's okay." I shook my head. "Keep going."

He dragged Grace out of Dad's office.

I took Dad's keys from his desk drawer and led Donny to part of the zoo that's usually locked up. It's where we keep all the transit cages and where quarantined animals live when they first come to the zoo. Grace calls that part of the zoo

"Backstage," like we're in some kind of theater—typical Grace, trying to make something sound glamorous when it's not. Anyway, Backstage was empty, so I figured it was the best place to hide a pack of werewolves.

Donny and I worked together to pile the sleeping wolves into one of the empty cages.

"How long before they wake up?" I asked, wiping sweat from my forehead with shaking hands—I was a wreck!

"Long enough to figure out what to do," Donny replied.

He ran his hands through his mop of gray hair and stared at the cage, deep in thought. I felt my eyebrows tighten together as I tried to figure out what he was thinking. Nothing about Donny made sense: Where had he come from? Why was he helping me?

"Who *are* you?" I asked him. "How did you know this was gonna happen?"

Donny turned and looked me in the eye, "I'll answer your questions, Sammy, I promise. But right now we need to make sure no one else finds out about this. Questions later, actions now. Okay?"

"How do I know I can trust you?" I held my breath, waiting for an answer.

"You don't." He shrugged. Not the answer I was looking for. "But right now, you don't have a choice."

He was right. I had no one else to turn to. All the other zookeepers had gone home, and even if they hadn't, they'd be as crazy as a surfing kangaroo to go anywhere near werewolves. That's if they even believed me.

Donny reeled off a list of orders for me to follow, like he was an army general and we were going to war.

I couldn't think—my brain felt as numb as a dead leg—but Donny knew exactly what to do. It was obvious he'd dealt with situations like this a bazillion times before.

So I did everything he asked.

I walked back to Dad's office and cleared away the clothes Mom, Dad, Grace and Natty had ripped through when they turned into werewolves. Then I swung by the lion-feed fridges and picked up as many raw steaks as I could carry. I took the meat Backstage and passed it to Donny, who tossed it into the cage.

Next I used Dad's cell phone to call Seb, the most senior zookeeper at Feral Zoo; he's been working here since before I was born.

"It's Sammy," I said into the phone, trying to sound as normal as possible.

"All right, Sammy," Seb replied. He sounded suspicious—and I'm not surprised—I've never called him before.

"Mom and Dad have taken Grace and Natty to visit Grandma Nancy for the weekend," I lied. "They've left me here so I can work on a school project."

"Ah," Seb muttered down the phone. "What project's that then?"

"I'm doing a science project on wolves," I told him. The cover story had sounded all right in my head. Out loud it sounded stupid. I scrunched my eyes shut and carried on talking, crossing all my fingers and toes in hope that Seb believed me. "Dad's arranged for some rare wolves to be locked up in one of the Backstage cages for me to study."

"Lucky you!" Seb chuckled over the phone.

It worked! Seb believed me! I should win an award for that performance!

After speaking to Seb I tried to find Donny. But he'd gone—no idea where.

I stuck around Backstage for a while, waiting for Donny to come back. But standing alone listening to a pack of werewolves snoring wasn't my idea of fun. So I headed to the reptile house to be with Beelzebub, and sat down to try to make sense of everything.

I'm still doing that now.

I can't sleep. My mind is racing like a motorcycle. So I'm writing this diary—I need something to do. I need to keep busy.

11 P.M.

I feel like a badger or a mole or a bat, or another animal that's awake all night long. I've never had a problem sleeping before—Mom's always said I sleep more than a giant sloth. What am I going to do? My life is never going to be the same again! What if they never turn back? Can you undo becoming a werewolf?

I haven't left the zoo.

Luckily I know loads of survival tips, like how to stay warm at night without a blanket (I found a roll of tin foil in the zoo café and have wrapped it around myself).

I'm going to visit the wolves again—maybe this has all just been a bad dream.

Will write again soon . . . hopefully with good news.

MIDNIGHT

Nope.

No good news.

It wasn't a dream.

My family are still werewolves.

After I went Backstage I sat and watched them sleeping.

Dad was the first to wake up. I rushed to the cage. "Dad, you okay?"

But all Dad did was bare his teeth and growl. Then he started thrashing around, howling and trying to get out of the cage. He was foaming at the mouth, and his eyes were wide and crazed. The strangest thing . . . between the bloodthirsty wolf noises, I thought I could hear his voice.

I thought I heard him saying something about being hungry.

I'm so tired that I'm imagining a werewolf spoke!

I never normally cry. Crying's for girls and babies. But at that moment I felt all the air squeeze out of my lungs and my eyes itched like mad.

I used to think it would be really cool if Mom and Dad just disappeared. I used to think I'd be free to eat what I want, stay up late and have adventures. But I don't think that now. I don't care about staying up late. All I care about is getting them back to normal. I'm worried they'll be stuck like this forever. What will happen to the zoo? What will happen to me?

1 A.M.

PS I helped myself to some fruit from the zoo café cos I was starving. I figure Dad wouldn't mind me stealing right now, especially healthy stuff like fruit.

3 A.M.

PPS Donny still hasn't come back. No idea where he is or even *who* he is. Will try calling him in the morning.

3:10 A.M.

PPPS I'm still starving. Fruit stinks.

Saturday April 4th

Sammy Feral = unlucky.

Yes, I'm sleeping in a zoo. Yes, I have no one to nag me about brushing my teeth. Yes, my pet python shed his skin this morning. But I have a pack of werewolves for relatives—and that totally outweighs all the good stuff.

I must have fallen asleep next to Beelzebub's tank. Max woke me up this morning when he came in to sweep the floor.

Max is Grace's boyfriend and a junior zookeeper. I used to think Max was cool—but a few months ago I was snooping in Grace's room and found a love letter he'd written. I don't wanna repeat any of it in case I puke all over my diary, but it was the soppiest, slushiest, girliest nonsense I've ever heard. I lost a lot of respect for Max that day.

"Up late last night talking to snakes?" Max joked as he swept the floor.

"Er, yeah," I replied, yawning.

Max leaned on his broom and stared at me suspiciously, "Seb told me your folks have gone away for a few days. Who's looking after you?"

"They've given me special permission to camp out here in the zoo," I lied. Max knew as well as I did that my parents only let me sleep over in the zoo on my birthday. And even then Dad sleeps in his office so I'm not here on my own. And my birthday is months away!

"Have you heard from them since they went?" Max asked.

I knew that when he said "them" he meant Grace.

"No. They're staying with Grandma Nancy. They're probably really busy," I said quickly.

Then Max tried to talk to me about a delivery of spider tanks that's due in, but I wasn't listening. All I could think about was checking on the werewolves. I hadn't seen them since last night. And who knows what kind of crazy could have gone down since then . . .

I made my way toward the reptile-house exit. The door swung open and Seb walked in with a scowl on his face.

"Your dad tell you how to shut those rare-breed wolves up?" he asked me, annoyed. "They won't stop yapping—they've been at it for hours. And I can't find the spare key for Backstage . . ."

"Er . . . don't worry about that," I said, panicking at the thought of Seb seeing the werewolves. "I'll go check on them. Sorry."

"Sorry won't feed those poor animals, lad.

Lucky your friends are here to help look after them or they'd all starve to death."

"My *friends?*" I asked, confused.

"The boy with the funny gray hair—he's here with a girl, said they were friends of yours . . ."

I didn't wait to hear any more. I ran out of the reptile house as fast as a lion charging toward a juicy antelope.

I bolted past the elephants, past Khan the Sumatran tiger, and around a bunch of zoo visitors taking pictures of Darwin the gorilla. I arrived at the Backstage gate and froze with fear.

Seb was right—the howling was so loud I could hardly think. It didn't sound like normal wolves— way too blood-curdling to be normal.

I fumbled with the key until the gate swung open.

Donny was standing in the Backstage yard throwing raw steaks through the cage bars. A girl with bright red hair was standing next to him. She wasn't helping—just standing with her arms crossed, glaring.

Was I pleased to see Donny? Does hippo poo stink? OF COURSE I WAS!

Finally, time to get some answers!

"Donny!" I shouted. "Man, am I pleased to see you. Who's your friend?"

"This is Red; she's here to help," Donny said as he narrowly avoided Natty biting his hand clean off.

"Sorry they're so hungry," I said feebly. "I haven't fed them since they woke up. I couldn't really face looking at them when . . ."

"Let's focus on the werewolves shall we, kid?" Red snapped at me. "Stop worrying about your emotional issues until there's no danger of us becoming wolf meat."

If my eyebrows rose any further up my head I'd be wearing them as a hat.

I was SPEECHLESS.

How rude was she?

RED

Age: Looks around 15

Job: Donny's sidekick

Looks like: A raccoon, thanks to black make-up. Hair as bright as a coral reef

First impressions: Moody, rude, arrogant, clearly doesn't like me

Er, who did Red think she was? My mind scrambled to find a witty comeback. But my brain was frazzled from lack of sleep and werewolf-induced shock. All I could do was clench my teeth and narrow my eyes in anger.

Not only is she rude, Red's as weird-looking as Donny. Seriously, she's not like any girl I've ever seen. She's got red hair and emo-goth-supreme black clothes and black lipstick and eye makeup. She had a large skull pendant around her neck—how morbid is that? What kind of freak train brought her into town?

"Hungry?" Donny smiled, bending down and opening a large bag.

The smell of greasy burger and fries wafted up my nose and my stomach growled with hunger. I quickly forgot about being annoyed at Red—eating was way more important.

I sat on the ground, with my back to the werewolf cage, and stuffed my face. After devouring my burger and fries I had more than a few questions for Donny, "Who are you? Why are you helping me? How did you know this was going to happen? Why didn't you stop it?"

Red rolled her eyes and muttered something under her breath. Donny ignored her and pushed his gray hair from his face, "Like my card says, I'm a cryptozoologist. You know what that means, Sammy?"

I nodded my head and recited what Dad had told me yesterday: "Someone who studies animals that don't exist. Like the abominable snowman, or dragons, or werewolves."

Red's eyes darted toward me and looked vaguely impressed. "But werewolves *do* exist," she pointed out. "As you can clearly see."

"Er, you think I don't know that?" I said. "Werewolves are as real as a hippo's bad breath!"

"I've been tracking a werepup dealer for a couple of months," Donny said, ignoring my brilliant comeback. "The dealer is the guy who sold Caliban to your father. I didn't know for sure that Caliban was a werepup—that's why I didn't act sooner. Lucky for you I was here at all— or every animal in the zoo would probably be wolf feed by now." Donny sounded like he was reading a weather report—like what he was saying was totally normal.

Well, it didn't sound normal to me. Caliban's

a werepup?! I thought back to all the times I'd run around the garden with him and tried to teach him tricks—all that time he'd been waiting to attack, waiting to kill, waiting to turn us into mutant killers!

I needed more answers. I needed to know how I could fix things.

"What now?" I eagerly asked Donny. "They can be fixed, right?"

Donny made a whistling sound through his teeth and said, "First we need to take fur samples."

"Why?" I asked, standing up and scrunching the trash from my meal into a small ball. "Shouldn't we be focusing on making the fur disappear?"

"I need to establish which breed of werewolf we're dealing with," Donny said, pulling an empty specimen jar from his pocket.

"And then we cure them?" I said hopefully.

"There's no such thing as a werewolf cure,"

Red grunted, as if I had just asked her to explain how to count to five.

Er, excuse me? Replay!

"WHAT?" I asked, stunned. Not possible. No way. Red was wrong. Had to be, *had to be*. The idea that my family could be stuck like this forever was unthinkable. "What do you mean?"

"He's not all that bright, is he?" Red smirked at Donny. "This is gonna be one long full moon if we have to explain every last—"

"Are you a cryptozoologist too?" I snapped at Red.

"No," she replied, offering no further explanation.

I'd already made up my mind that Red was the most miserable person I'd ever, ever met.

If Red wasn't a cryptozoologist, then she obviously knew nothing about werewolves. And if she knows nothing about werewolves, then how can she know there's no such thing as a cure? Er, she can't! She's talking nonsense! "If you don't know anything about werewolves," I said, "then why are you here?"

Red raised an arched eyebrow and gave me a knowing smirk.

"Watch this," Donny said. He pulled his silver blowpipe out of his ripped jeans pocket and, in the blink of an eye, shot the five wolves with darts from the pipe. They each fell to the ground with a thud.

"Are you sure that won't hurt them?" I winced, hearing the thunk of Dad's teeth clashing against the cage bars as he collapsed.

Donny shrugged. "There's no other way to get near a werewolf safely."

I pointed at the cage lock. "I left the key in—"

"No keys needed." Red grinned with a mischievous glint in her eyes.

I shuffled my weight between my feet nervously, waiting for Red to reach between the cage bars. But that's not what she did.

Red stood completely still—I couldn't even see her breathing.

She stared hard at some of the bars of the cage. Her eyes bored into the metal as if she was telling it something with her mind. I felt the air around me begin to tremble like the hum of distant thunder, and the hairs on the back of my neck stood to attention. Then something amazing happened: the cage bars began to bend. Yep, Red was bending metal with the power of her mind.

Two metal bars pulled apart with a heavy groan, creating a gap wide enough to walk through.

My mouth hung open as wide as a bear den. "What the . . . ? How did you . . . ?"

"Questions later," Red interrupted.

"Quick, before they wake up," Donny whispered, stepping between the bent bars into the cage. He was totally unfazed by what had just happened—as if bending solid metal with the power of your mind was as normal as eating lunch.

I watched Donny and Red crouch down and cut small patches of fur from the sleeping werewolves' necks. They carefully put the fur samples into specimen jars and labeled them. When they'd finished they walked out of the cage and Red stared at the cage bars until they went back to how they were before.

For the record, bending metal with your mind

is possibly the most AMAZING trick ever. Shame it's only Red that can do it. I wonder if she can teach me?

"We'll be back by nightfall," Donny muttered as they walked away from me. "Remember to feed the wolves this time."

"Wait . . . you can't leave me here again . . ." But Donny and Red didn't stick around to listen.

You think that part of my day was weird? That cryptozoologists, girls bending metal with their mind, and werewolves are weird? Well, it gets weirder.

My life is a whole new breed of crazy . . .

I hung around Backstage watching my were-family sleeping.

Once again Dad was the first to wake up. He pulled his heavy wolf body up and arched his back. Slowly, like he was stalking prey, wolf-Dad walked over to the cage bars and glared at me. Then I heard him talk.

That's right, I heard a werewolf speak . . .

"If I wasn't in this cage I'd be eating you for lunch . . ."

I was flabbergasted. He might be a werewolf, but how could my own dad say something like that to me?

What did he say next? Well, you're as crazy as a cockroach in a party hat if you think I stuck around to hear more. I ran away as fast as I could. I sprinted all the way to the reptile house without looking back once. I shut the door behind me, sank to the floor, and waited for Donny to get back.

7:30 P.M.

Donny and Red got back just after sunset. Once again I felt like doing a jig of joy when I saw Donny appear. Let's face it—I'd be sunk without him.

"I thought I'd find you here," Donny said, as I

opened the door to let him in. "Things at the lab took longer than expected."

He handed me a bag of potato chips, which I tore open and started eating without even saying thank you—I was S.T.A.R.V.I.N.G!

"So, give me the news," I said, without stopping to ask what kind of teenager has access to a lab that tests werewolf fur. "What kind of werewolves are we dealing with? Obviously they're the kind that speak—"

"Speak?" Red interrupted with a raised eyebrow.

"Yeah. After you left," I explained, "Dad woke up and spoke to me. He said he'd be eating me for lunch if he wasn't locked in a cage."

Donny and Red exchanged a confused look.

"What?" I said, wiping potato chip crumbs from my chin.

"Sammy, werewolves can't speak," Donny said.

"Yes, they can," I argued. "The werewolf didn't

sound like my dad—he sounded like a talking wolf—but he definitely spoke."

Donny slowly paced toward me, locking my gaze into his. "Sammy, I don't know what you heard, but it wasn't your dad. Maybe you're tired; maybe you should eat a proper meal—"

"I know what I heard!" I shouted. I didn't mean to shout at Donny—he was the last person I wanted to argue with.

"Prove it," Red said, folding her arms across her chest.

Fine, I will! I thought—and I'm gonna love proving Red wrong!

I led Donny and Red out of the reptile house, around the zoo and through the Backstage gates.

The sound of the werewolves' howling was louder than a choir of elephants. Through the howls I could hear words. And it wasn't just Dad I could hear this time—I could hear everyone, even Caliban . . .

"Here they come again . . ."

"We could turn them . . ."

"Make them just like us. One bite is all it would take . . ."

I looked at Donny and Red. "Can't you hear that?" I said in astonishment.

"Hear what?" Donny looked really worried for me—he must have thought I was crazy!

But I'm not crazy—and I was gonna prove it.

I listened hard, and carefully repeated every last word I could hear: "'One bite is all it would take' to turn us into werewolves."

Red drew in a deep breath and Donny's eyes looked as though they were going to pop out of his head and roll around the floor.

"What did you say?" Donny whispered. "How do you know that they could turn us with just one bite?"

"I told you," I said. "They're speaking—and that's what they're saying."

"The lab tests confirmed that we're dealing with Celest werewolves." Donny stared at me thoughtfully. "Celests have the most infectious bite of any species of wolf. It only takes one bite to turn someone."

"Look, I don't know what you mean by 'Celest' wolves," I replied. "But I can understand what they're saying. Now do you believe me?"

"Maybe the kid's not so boring after all." Red eyed me with suspicion. "Maybe he's a CSC?"

"Maybe." Donny nodded.

"A what?" I asked.

"A Cross-Species Communicator," Donny explained. "Has this ever happened before?"

"Have I ever had a conversation with a werewolf before? Er, no." I shook my head.

"Have you spoken to any animal before?" Red asked seriously.

"Sure," I answered. "But they never talk back."

"Interesting," Donny said with delight. He looked like someone who'd just discovered a new planet, he seemed so pleased with himself. "You're more special than I thought, Sammy."

Me? Special? Er, I don't think so. Up until yesterday my life had been nothing but normal.

"I'm not special," I told him. "I'm just a regular twelve-year-old whose life has suddenly strolled into wackoville. You're right, maybe I am just imagining stuff. I am really tired."

Donny stared at me some more. "I'll run some tests on you tomorrow," he said.

Tests? What am I now, some kind of science experiment? The last thing I want is for Donny to waste time doing tests on me while everyone I care about is locked up in a cage!

And besides, what if Donny's tests show that there's something seriously wrong with me? Maybe I'm slowly turning into a werewolf too, and that's why I can understand them.

It's all such a mess. How am I ever going to make things right again?

Sunday April 5th

I slept in the reptile house again last night.

When I woke up I saw Donny peering into Sid the cobra's tank. Honestly, Donny is one crazy dude—I've never met anyone like him before.

Other than a few dozen snakes, we were totally alone—a perfect opportunity to get some answers! So I asked Donny to tell me everything he knew about werewolves. He told me loads.

Now I know enough about werewolves to start writing a book about them . . .

Sammy Feral's Guide to Werewolves

Chapter 1: An Introduction to Werewolves

* A werewolf is an animal infected with the Were Virus.
* Once infected, an animal turns into a werewolf for three days each month, from the night before to the night after the full moon.
* There are over a million known werewolves worldwide.
* It's Donny's job to keep werewolves a secret.

Before I could ask Donny anything else, Red came into the reptile house with three hot chocolates and warm muffins for breakfast.

"You'll have to entertain yourself today, kid," Red said, biting into a blueberry muffin.

I frowned. "For the record, I hate being called 'kid'."

Red rolled her eyes and took a huge bite of her muffin. She's almost, *almost*, as annoying as Grace is—only Grace is my sister so she gets away with it. Red has no excuse, she's just a Miss Crabbypants.

"We're going to pick up a few more things to set up shop here," Donny explained.

"Set up shop?" I repeated, confused.

"We figured a squirt like you can't cope with five werewolves by yourself—so we're gonna stick around and help out for a while." Red smirked. It was almost as if she was trying to annoy me.

"It's our job to help people like you," Donny agreed, taking a slurp of hot chocolate.

"Who employs you?" I asked.

"We work for ourselves," Red said bluntly.

"Besides," Donny winked at me, "you'd be doing me a favor if you let me stick around and do some research into that talent of yours."

Red snorted at the word "talent." I guess speaking to werewolves is pretty boring to someone who can bend metal with her mind.

"Sure." I shrugged. No way did I want Donny to do tests on me—but I was as happy as a warthog in mud that he was sticking around.

Donny and Red left the zoo after breakfast.

After quickly throwing in steaks for the werewolves, I avoided being anywhere near them. Seeing Mom, Dad, Grace, and Natty like that just makes me sad.

Fingers crossed they'll be back to normal when the full moon ends tomorrow. I can't stop thinking about what life will be like if they're gone forever. No more watching nature documentaries with Dad, no more of Mom's amazing homemade burgers, no little sister to annoy, no big sister to embarrass. That's the kind of stuff that makes life great—without it, everything just seems pointless.

I spent the rest of the morning with Max. I was pleased to have some company—even if all Max ever talks about is Grace. Total barf-fest!!

Max and I swept out the baboon enclosure, groomed the llamas (which made me miss Mom loads), and fed the elephants—all before lunch.

I got a text from my best friend Mark as I was munching a cheese sandwich in the zoo café at lunchtime.

Wanna hang out @ mine 2nite?
Dad's workin l8 & Mom's cooking spaghetti.

There's nothing I want more than to eat spaghetti (I'd wrestle a bear for a proper meal right now) and hang out with Mark as if everything's normal. But everything isn't normal. No way can I leave the zoo while everyone I care about is walking on all fours.

I texted back:

Can't 2nite. Soz.

My phone beeped again. But the text wasn't from Mark, it was from Donny.

@ Backstage gates.
In van with pets.
Let me in

Pets?

I took the rest of my lunch to eat on the way and went to let Donny in. He parked his big white van in the Backstage yard.

"*You're looking tasty today, little brother,*" Grace snarled as I walked past their cage.

I shuddered and tried to ignore her.

"I thought we could camp out in there." Donny pointed. At the back of the Backstage yard is a small building with two offices and a kitchen—no one ever really uses it.

"Sure," I replied, trying to ignore Mom whispering death threats through the cage bars. "What's this about pets?"

Donny flashed me a knowing grin. "I don't set up shop anywhere without my pets—they come everywhere with me. Help me bring them inside?"

Red swung open the van door and passed me a small tank.

I nearly dropped the whole thing on the floor and screamed. Not in a bazillion years could you guess what was looking up at me . . .

A three-headed snake.

Yep, that's right—freakoid snake supreme.

"Are you my lunch?" it hissed up at me. *"Could be fatter . . . but you'll do!"*

What's the deal with everyone wanting to eat me?! NOT COOL!!

"Er, no," I stuttered at the snake. "You don't wanna eat me."

"What did you say?" Donny looked at me strangely.

"Nothing," I replied. "Just telling your pet here that I'm not on the lunch menu."

"Looks like it's not just werewolves freak-boy can talk to." Red grinned at Donny.

"Don't call me freak-boy," I shouted as I walked away toward the offices. "If you wanna see a freak, then look in the mirror!"

Red laughed as I walked into the building and let the door slam behind me.

I spent the next few hours helping move Donny's "pets" into the Backstage offices.

Here are just a couple of the freaky animals he has:

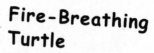

Phoenix

A bird that bursts into flames and is then born again from the ashes. Mega-cool.

Fire-Breathing Turtle

Spits fire into the air. Looks like a half-dragon, half-turtle.

"Red, you sure you can't hear that?" I asked, staring into freakoid snake's tank.

"Hear what?" She rolled her eyes at me. "The sound of my brain cells dying as I listen to your dumb questions?"

I don't know why I bother talking to Red.

"What is it?" I asked, turning to Donny and pointing at the three-headed snake.

"Gut worm," he replied. Like I should have recognized a gut worm.

I inspected the creature closely. Each head had a pair of sharp fangs and cold reptilian eyes. "Usually I love snakes, but these guys are something else. They keep asking me to open their cage and let them out."

"NO!" Donny shouted.

"Don't worry—I wasn't going to," I assured him.

"The last thing we need is an escaped gut worm slithering around," Donny said seriously.

"They'll rip your guts open and climb in," Red said, with the faintest hint of a smile on her black-painted lips.

"What are the others saying?" Donny asked, dumping a large suitcase on to the floor.

I approached the fire-breathing turtle, "Well, this guy—"

"His name's Nim," Donny interrupted, tapping

on the glass of the tank. "Fire-breathing turtles are very rare, you know. He's one of the last of his kind."

"He doesn't speak much," I told Donny.

"Well, Sammy, now we know for sure that you're a CSC." Donny sighed, as if speaking to gut worms was as normal as learning to crawl. "Only with you, it seems you can only speak to rare animals: werewolves, gut worms . . ."

Whoa, rewind . . . life just got a little crazier! A couple of days ago I thought werewolves and phoenixes were just make-believe—and now, not only do they exist, but I can speak to them!?

So Donny was right, I was "special." But I'm not sure I want to be special—not if it involves being able to speak to werewolves. Can't I bend metal with my mind instead?

"So what should I do now?" I asked, confused.

"You can talk to the animals I spend my life

working with," Donny said thoughtfully. "You could be useful to have around."

Red made a loud grunting noise. Clearly she wasn't happy at the thought of me crashing her and Donny's freak party for two.

"I like collecting weirdos." Donny smiled at me.

"I'm no weirdo," I said defensively.

"Sammy," Donny said as he pulled a bag of food pellets from his suitcase and dropped them into

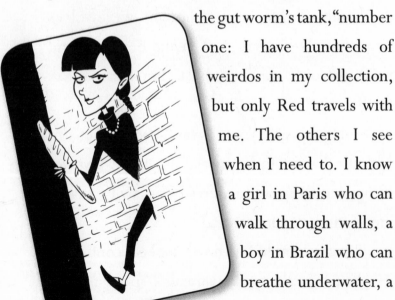

the gut worm's tank, "number one: I have hundreds of weirdos in my collection, but only Red travels with me. The others I see when I need to. I know a girl in Paris who can walk through walls, a boy in Brazil who can breathe underwater, a girl who can travel through dreams, the list goes on. And number two, you are a weirdo, Sammy, you just haven't admitted it yet. Once you do, I promise life will get easier."

"What about other werewolves?" I asked, an idea brewing in my head. "Do you know any others?"

"Of course," Donny laughed. "Not many in this country though— the Were Virus isn't that widespread here. The nearest werewolf, Dr. Lycan, lives a few hundred miles away."

"Can I speak to him?" Excitement bubbled inside me.

Donny's smile dropped from his face and he grew serious, "Why?"

"I just think it would help to speak to someone who's been through the whole full-moon thing before. Maybe they could help me find a cure."

Red huffed air loudly through her nostrils, "Seriously, kid, you need to let go of this whole 'cure' idea you've got going on. Read my lips: NEVER GONNA HAPPEN!"

I ignored Red and her painted black lips. "Donny, please?"

"Sure," he agreed, and scribbled down an e-mail address on a scrap of paper. "Just don't go getting your hopes up. And don't expect a reply while the moon is still full."

I had the e-mail address of another real-life werewolf. And a doctor, too—that means he must be majorly smart. Result! Maybe now I could get some advice on a werewolf cure, since all Donny and Red can do is keep telling me there isn't one.

Donny and Red spent the next few hours making the Backstage offices into their new home. I was impressed by how much stuff they'd brought with them: cots, sleeping bags, food (for them and the pets), and hundreds of books. There were books about all kinds of crazy animals, including werewolves, as well as school textbooks for math, history and science. "They're mine," Red snapped at me as I went to put the school books in Donny's room.

All right, moody! Don't bother asking for help next time!

Donny lent me his computer while he was unpacking. I logged into my e-mail account and sent Dr. Lycan a message.

Hi,

My name's Sammy Feral and my mom, dad, and two sisters have just been turned into Celest werewolves. I need to find a way to cure them.

I hear you're a werewolf too. Can you help me?

I'm only 12 years old so I can't pay you very much money. But my family owns a zoo—Feral Zoo—and I can promise you lifelong free admission for you and all your friends and family if you can help.

Please write back as soon as possible.

Thank you very much,

Sammy Feral

As it grew dark outside, the wolves began to howl loudly. I've noticed they get extra touchy at nighttime.

Tonight's the last night of the full moon. Fingers crossed that when I wake up tomorrow everyone will be normal again.

I HAVE to find a way to make things better. No way do I want to deal with a pack of werewolves once a month! I have to find a cure. Just because no one's ever found a cure before doesn't mean that one doesn't exist. And I'm going to be the one who finds it!

Monday April 6th

Best news since the discovery of the Ninja Frog: the Woof Brigade are human again!

Honestly, I'd have hair as gray as Donny's if I had to deal with werewolves for a second longer.

Last night I spent the whole night sitting by the werewolves' cage. I wanted to be there when they turned back. I watched as they prowled around until the sun started to come up, then one by one they laid down on the ground and fell asleep.

I must have fallen asleep too cos I woke up with a blanket over me. It was bright daylight and Red and Donny were passing clothes through the cage bars (my family had all been naked since ripping their clothes when they first turned into werewolves).

Thank goodness for Donny thinking ahead and bringing clothes. If the sight of Mom and Dad as werewolves wasn't enough to bring on a heart attack, looking at their bare butts would have made me keel over for sure!

I sprung to my feet like an excited kangaroo and rushed over to the cage. Donny unlocked the cage door and everyone sheepishly walked out.

"Mom! You're back!" I beamed as I threw my arms around her. I clung to her tightly; it felt so good to hug her.

But she didn't hug me back. Her arms hung limply at her sides.

I took a step back and looked her in the eyes. She blinked vacantly, like she didn't even see me.

My heart sank to the zoo floor. This was the worst feeling in the world. Why wasn't she pleased to see me?

I looked around at Dad, Grace, and Natty, but none of them even smiled at me. It was like I didn't exist. Natty was cradling Caliban in her arms as if he was a doll—even he seemed to have had the life sucked out of him.

"They'll need to sleep for the rest of the day, Sammy," Donny said gently. I think he could see how bummed out I was. "It's normal for werewolves to be exhausted at the end of the full moon."

Exhausted?

Not an excuse, sorry!

The least they could have done is thank me for keeping them safe—and for keeping all the zoo animals safe—but they didn't say anything. It made me feel so angry—all this time I've busted a gut trying to hold everything together, and I don't even get a "thank you!"

Donny drove me and the ex-wolves home in his van.

Sure enough, everyone went straight to bed. Without a single word.

I tried to think about what Donny had said—that they were exhausted and just needed to rest. Dad's eye bags *were* twice their normal size. But I can't help feeling a bit cheated—it hasn't exactly been the reunion I was hoping for.

I jumped in the shower (I stank of zoo) and got into my school uniform. Putting on my school clothes felt weird—my life has changed so much since the last time I wore them.

Feral family mornings are usually full of noise. But the only sound this morning was everyone snoring. It wasn't right. I've never felt so lonely in all my life.

Last year in geography we learned about the Richter scale. The Richter scale was invented by a guy called Charles Richter and it measures the size of earthquakes from 1 to 10 (1 is small and 10 is mega). Well, I've decided to start my own scale—it's going to be called the "Feral Scale of Weirdness." I'm going to use it to measure just how crazy something is. The last few days officially register as a solid 9.

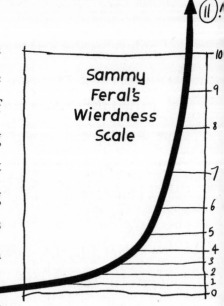

Sammy Feral's Wierdness Scale

Why haven't I awarded it a full 10? Because I have a sneaky suspicion that things are going to get even weirder . . .

9 P.M.

Just had the worst day in the history of everything.

I really didn't think things could get much worse. Turns out I was wrong. Even if someone offered me a zoo full of rare-breed snakes, I still wouldn't live today again—it stunk!

I had major brain freeze this morning and forgot to meet Mark at the school gates (something I've done every single day since we started school).

MARK

Job: My best friend

Looks like: A cheeky monkey with the hair of an unbrushed terrier

Age: 12

Can be found: Looking after his pet iguana and telling the worst jokes EVER!

Favorite animal: Komodo dragons

Mrs. Brown called Mark's name from the class list and no one answered. I knew right away that was

because he was still waiting for me outside the school gates.

"You're late," grumbled Mrs. Brown when Mark eventually walked in.

"Sorry," he apologized, sitting down next to me. "I waited half an hour for you," he whispered angrily. "Where were you?"

"I just . . . forgot," I mumbled.

Mark looked at me, waiting for more of an explanation, but I didn't say anything. What was I supposed to say? *Sorry, Mark, I was way too busy thinking about death-by-werewolves.* I don't think so—that would be more disastrous than marrying an elephant.

The rest of the day didn't get any better:

* I totally flunked my math test (hadn't done any studying over the weekend).
* I forgot to bring in my history homework (not that I'd done it).

✱   I dropped my lunch tray on the floor and spilled water all over my pants so it looked like I'd wet myself. I was the laughingstock of the lunch hall.

All day long my eyes were totally glazing over and I felt like I could have slept for a bazillion years—I was so tired.

I've never been so happy to hear the end-of-school bell in my life!

"Yo, Sammy!" Mark called, catching up to me at the school gates. "Check out this joke I just made up in geography: Why did the spider buy a new car?"

I ignored Mark and kept on walking; I was mega-tired and not in the mood for bad jokes.

"So he could take it for a spin!" Mark said proudly, laughing at himself. "What you up to now? Wanna hang out at the zoo and feed the lions?"

"Don't really feel like going to the zoo tonight," I told him.

Mark looked at me as if I'd just told him I wanted to kiss a warthog. "What's up with you today?" he asked. "It's like you've eaten a three-course meal of weirdness."

I walked off without saying anything. If only Mark knew how right he was—not only have I eaten a three-course meal of weirdness, I've had a side order of crazy and a loony smoothie to wash it all down!

As I carried on walking, my phone beeped in my pocket. A text. I thought it was gonna be Mark, giving me grief about walking off. But the text wasn't from Mark, it was from Donny.

Spoke 2 yr folks 2day—
they know everything.
No secrets.

Er, not exactly sure what Donny meant by "No secrets." Did he mean Mom and Dad knew they were werewolves? Do they know about Red's powers? Do they know about mine?

As soon as I walked through the front door Caliban jumped up and gave me a huge lick on the cheek. I used to think it was cool that dogs are always so happy to see you. Now I'd rather join a boy band with three grizzly bears than let Caliban lick my face.

Before I'd even taken my coat off Mom ran to me and squeezed me so hard I couldn't breathe.

"Mom!" I wheezed.

"Sorry," she said, letting go of me and kissing my forehead. "I'm just so sorry, Sammy."

"It's okay," I said, grinning wildly. Man, was I pleased to have Mom back! "Are the others all right?"

"Yes." She sniffed. She looked as though she'd been crying.

I walked into the living room and Grace threw her arms around me, nearly squishing me to death. Seriously, Grace NEVER hugs me—so I knew for sure that she was mega-sorry.

"I'm so sorry I tried to kill you," she sobbed. "I didn't mean to . . . it's just . . ." I couldn't understand what else she was saying—there was some major supersonic whimpering going on.

"Darling, it's okay," Mom assured Grace, pulling her off me and sitting her down on the sofa. "Sammy knows you didn't mean it."

Do I? Grace made a pretty convincing killer werewolf, if you ask me!

"Caliban turned us into wolves," Natty said miserably. "I don't wanna be a wolf."

Dad picked Natty up and she buried her head into his shoulder and sobbed.

"Thank you, Sammy," Dad said gratefully with a huge smile. One of his front teeth was missing—he must have knocked it out when his faced slammed into the cage bars the other day. It looks really stupid.

But I don't care what he looks like. Having Dad back is better than a million Christmases rolled into one.

We spent the rest of the evening talking. I don't think we've ever just sat down and talked so much. They told me about what it's like to be a werewolf—apparently they now have super-senses of hearing and smell and just wanna eat raw meat the whole time, even when they're not wolves.

When it was time to go to bed I went up to my room and turned on my computer. I logged into my e-mail account—I wanted to see if Dr. Lycan had e-mailed me back.

Nothing.

Bummed out.

Dr. Werewolf is pretty much the best shot I have of finding a cure. But I guess there are other things I could do that might help . . .

* Do some Internet research.
* Read through the dusty old books on Donny's bookshelf looking for clues.
* Learn more about the lunar cycle.
* Cross my fingers and hope . . .

Tuesday April 7th

I skipped going to the zoo after school again today so I could do some werewolf Internet research. Obviously the first thing I typed into the search engine was "werewolf cure."

A split second later I had 8,987 hits. Things were looking good. But as I started to check out the sites I realized that most of them had clearly been written by crazies who'd never even met a real-life werewolf. Nonsense!

As my heart sank I clicked on one more site . . . Result!

I punched the air with excitement when I read that there are FIVE possible werewolf cures.

Five! Donny and Red can bow down and call me "King"—clearly they were wrong; there *is* such a thing as a werewolf cure.

Check this out:

1 Don't get bitten

2 Kneeling in the same spot for 100 years

3 Hearing your name called three times

4 Ingesting silver

5 Death

Okay, so cures number 2 and 5 are a bit drastic. And cure number 1 annoyed me—it's hardly a cure, is it? But maybe I could give the others a try.

I left my room and heard music blasting out of Grace's bedroom. Time to give number 3 a shot . . .

"Grace Lily Feral," I called, using her full name for extra effect. "Grace Lily Feral," I shouted louder.

Grace's music died down and she stomped toward her bedroom door.

Time to get in the third and final blow: "Grace Lily Feral."

"WHAT?" Grace shouted, swinging open her door and glaring.

"Feel any different?" I asked. "Less wolfy?"

"Urgh, you are SUCH a freak!" She rolled her eyes and slammed the door in my face.

Hmmm, I couldn't tell if it had worked or not.

I stalked outside Grace's room for a while, waiting to see what might happen.

"Sammy," she screamed above her music, "I can smell you outside my room. Bug off or you'll be sorry!"

Busted!

Well, cure number 3 was officially a dead end. No way could non-wolf Grace smell me from behind a closed door.

Maybe I'll have better luck with cure number 4? But how can I persuade someone to eat silver? This is gonna take some thought . . .

Wednesday April 8th

The dial on the Feral Scale of Weirdness was cranked up a notch or two today . . . and there's more evidence that I need to find a werewolf cure FAST!

The proof?

Hamster murder.

I came back from a lousy day at school to find Natty playing with Harry on the living-room floor. She'd put some kind of stupid hat on him and was driving him around the room in a remote-controlled car. That kind of stuff is animal cruelty, if you ask me . . .

Anyway, Caliban was lying on the sofa and

watching lazily, and I went into the kitchen to get myself a snack. That's when I heard Natty scream.

I ran back into the living room. The remote-control car was lying on its side and Natty was cradling Harry.

"Caliban bit him!" she cried. "He tried to eat Harry."

Caliban was still sprawled out on the sofa, though his ears twitched at the sound of his name. Blood was oozing from Harry's neck—there was no way he was gonna make it.

"Give him to me," I said to Natty. She passed Harry over—he was as dead as a dodo.

"Can you fix him?" Natty sobbed. It was then that I noticed the drops of hamster blood around Natty's mouth.

You don't have to be a detective to work out that it wasn't Caliban who killed Harry.

"I don't think he can be fixed, Natty," I said,

trying to sound kind. Natty let out a wail louder than a trumpeting elephant.

Later that evening we held a little funeral for Harry in the back garden. We buried him in between Chi-Chi the spaniel, who died crossing the road last year, and Petal (stupid name), the rabbit who was half eaten by a fox.

Natty cried all evening. She only had one raw sausage for dinner she was so upset.

I was so tired that I went to bed early, but Natty's howling was stopping me going to sleep. So I got up and went to see if she was okay.

"I miss Harry," she sobbed into her pillow dramatically.

"Want to see my dried toad collection?" I said, trying to cheer her up. She didn't respond. "What about my shark tooth?" Still nothing. "Dog biscuits?"

Natty looked up and gave me a big toothy grin, "Yes, please."

Having a sister who murders hamsters and eats dog biscuits is never good. There has to be some way I can fix this. If eating silver is the only hope of a werewolf cure, then maybe it's time to give it a try. I'll go to the zoo tomorrow and speak to Donny about the best way to go about it . . .

9:30 P.M.

Have texted Donny to tell him I'm coming to the zoo tomorrow to discuss werewolf cures. He texted back saying this:

> No such thing as a cure. But I want 2 talk about that talent of yours

Donny can talk about my CSC "talent" all he wants. But I still don't believe there's no such thing as a cure . . . I'm so gonna prove him wrong.

10:30 P.M.

Interesting development to report . . .

I couldn't sleep—too much going on inside my head—so I decided to turn on my computer and check my e-mails.

Dr. Lycan the werewolf has e-mailed me back . . .

Dear Sammy Feral,

I'm very sorry to hear that your family is sick. There's nothing I can do to help. Please don't contact me again.

Dr. L. Lycan

Nonsense!

I read the e-mail five times—I couldn't believe it.

Why doesn't Dr. Lycan want to speak to me? Other than Donny and Red, Dr. Wolf was the only person I could ask about this stuff.

I am not going to give up! Since when did giving up win a war?

And it is a war I'm fighting:

Me vs. Werewolves.

And if I don't win, then pretty soon hamster murder will be the least of my worries!

I'm going to visit Dr. Lycan, with or without an invitation!

Thursday April 9th

Forget the Feral Scale of Weirdness . . . how about the Feral Scale of Crappiness? And today is off the scale!

Let me explain . . .

Mark came to the zoo after school with me today. It's been ages since we hung out properly—so he came along to help me feed the snakes.

"I've persuaded Mom to let me have my birthday party at the zoo," he told me, as he stroked Beelzebub. Knowing Mark's folks, Mark must have done some world-class begging. His parents are both doctors and they've never liked him hanging out at the zoo—they're totally paranoid about him picking up weird animal diseases.

I quickly calculated in my head that Mark's birthday didn't clash with the full moon. "That's cool," I told him.

"Got any of those frozen field mice we could feed Beelzebub?" Mark asked, looking around.

"They're in the feeding fridges," I answered, seeing my opportunity to slip away so I could speak to Donny. "I'll go get some."

I know it sounds bad, but I couldn't wait to get away. Yeah, Mark's my best friend—but all I really wanted to do was go Backstage and talk to Donny. I was desperate to pick his brains about werewolves eating silver. And if Donny couldn't help me, then surely Dr. Lycan could. But Dr. Lycan doesn't want to see me. Plus I don't know where he lives.

But I'd bet a year's supply of frozen field mice that Donny does . . .

So I left Mark in the reptile house and headed Backstage. I did mean to go right back to Mark, honestly, but after what happened next, my best friend was the last thing on my mind . . .

Before I even got to the Backstage gates Red's bright head of hair sprung up out of nowhere. "Sammy, I need to speak to you," she said urgently.

"I'm busy," I snapped at her. "Unless it's about a werewolf cure?" I added hopefully.

Red shook her head and grabbed my arm to stop me marching away. "Your dad's selling the zoo," Red blurted.

I swung around and gave Red a death-stare. "Is this some sort of sick joke?"

"No, Sammy," she said seriously.

Er, rewind . . . what?

Dad was selling the zoo? Suddenly it felt like the whole world had stopped turning. Dad selling the zoo would be the WORST THING EVER!!!

"The man who's trying to buy the zoo is here," Red said quickly—she sounded really stressed. "He's in your dad's office right now. Donny and I know him." There was real fear in her eyes as she spoke. "He's bad news, Sammy. His name's Professor Pickitt. He's a cryptozoologist too. But he's not like Donny—he doesn't want to help animals; he wants to use them to make himself rich."

"How?" I asked.

"By creating a zoo full of 'mythical' animals like werewolves. He wants to lock people like your family in cages and charge the public to come and stare," she said bluntly.

"Why Feral Zoo?" I asked in panic. "And why now?"

"Exactly," Red said. "Something's up—and we need to find out what. Donny's on the case—he's with your dad and Pickitt now. I just thought I'd let you know."

She sounded embarrassed at the last part—like she hated the fact that she was doing me a favor.

"Thanks, Red."

We both ran through the zoo to Dad's office. We could hear three voices arguing inside the room: Dad's, Donny's, and one I didn't know—Pickitt's presumably.

I reached forward to open the office door, but Red blasted it open with her mind. Everyone stopped talking as we burst into the room.

"You must be Sammy Feral," snarled Professor Pickitt. He was small and greasy-looking, with oily hair, a pinstripe suit, and eyes that twitched like a small bird's.

PROFESSOR PICKITT

Age: Older than Mom and Dad

Job: Evil cryptozoologist

Looks like: A grin as sly as a cobra lying in wait

First impression: Bad news!!!

Just looking at Pickitt made me so angry I wanted to explode. "Who do you think you are?" I demanded. "What makes you think you can just stroll into our zoo and buy it? It's been in the Feral family for generations!"

Pickitt's mouth curled into a satisfied grin as he spoke. "I know what your father is, Sammy. He's a werewolf. And so's your mother, and your sisters too. And if you don't sell me the zoo, I'll tell the world."

"It's not true," I lied desperately. "You're crazy—there's no such thing as werewolves!" The hairs on the back of my neck were standing on end like a hedgehog at war. "I'd leave now, if I were you! This zoo is not for sale."

"I don't think you understand, Sammy." The professor grinned, his eyes blinking like crazy—he was sick in the head or something! "I always get what I want."

"That's enough!" Donny shouted. "You need to leave—now!"

Professor Pickitt's eyes lit up like a glaring campfire. "I'll be back," he said quietly. "I won't stop until I have what I want. This zoo is exactly what I've been looking for. People will travel from every corner of the world to point and stare at creatures like you, Mr. Feral. You won't stop me. No one can stop me!"

Without another word he turned and left.

I looked around the room in shock, waiting

for someone else to speak. But everyone was silent.

Dad looked like he'd already given up—like he just wanted the whole thing to be over. "Maybe selling the zoo would be for the best . . . after what's happened to us, I'm not sure we're the best people to run a zoo," he said—his eyes were as large as a raccoon's; I could tell he felt bad. "Unless, we *can* find a cure—"

"I'll find a cure," I said quickly. "I've already started researching it, and—"

"Sammy, it can't be done." Donny shook his head.

"Right about that," agreed Red.

No, not right. Wrong, wrong, wrong!

"What do you know?" I fumed at Red. "Listen, Donny," I pleaded. "I've read something on the Internet about werewolves ingesting silver . . ."

"It doesn't work, Sammy," Donny said firmly. "Trust me. I know a dozen werewolves that have tried that trick, and not one of them has been cured. You need to drop the whole 'werewolf cure' obsession and start being realistic. And we need to have a serious talk about that talent of yours—"

"Talent!" I shouted so loudly I made everyone jump. "It's not a talent, it's a curse! And unless it's going to stop Dad selling the zoo, then I couldn't care less about it."

Dad came toward me, his hands outstretched. "Sammy, calm down."

Calm down? Er I don't think so somehow!

I stumbled backward, shaking my head in disbelief. I didn't want to listen to another word. No way am I prepared to accept that there's no such thing as a werewolf cure. No way can my family stay like this forever! No way can Dad sell the zoo to Professor Pickitt!

I stormed off. I walked all the way home without looking back. I was SO angry!

My mind is made up: I'm going to find a cure, no matter what.

9 P.M.

Just got this text from Mark:

> I waited hours 4 u.
> Where u go? I'll come 2
> the zoo again 2morrow
> after skl—we can sort
> out stuff 4 my party!

I haven't texted back. The last thing I can think about when Dad's gonna sell the zoo is Mark's party! If only Mark knew the truth. I can't tell him now, no way. I'm in far too deep—he'll never understand.

Friday April 10th

Couldn't face going to the zoo after school today. Instead I spent hours on the Web searching for a way to cure werewolves. Didn't find anything new.

Just before dinner Grace came into my room without knocking. She was holding something in her hand, "Hey, freckle-face, forgotten who your friends are?" She was still wearing her zoo clothes—usually Grace won't be seen dead in zoo clothes when she's not at the zoo, but this last week she's become a total crudmuffin. I guess her standards have slipped since becoming a werewolf.

"Huh?" I gawped at her. Her eyes were red. I think she'd been crying. "You been blubbering about being a wolf again, Grace?"

Should not have said that.

She threw what she was holding on to the floor and stamped her foot in rage. "You'd cry too if you had to pluck hair from your ears!"

She stormed off. I heard her bedroom door slam as I picked up what she'd thrown on my floor—it was a letter, addressed to me.

I opened the envelope. It was a note written in Mark's handwriting.

Sammy,

I guess you forgot you were supposed to help me plan my birthday
party in the zoo today. I didn't see
you after school so I turned up at
the zoo and waited for ages. I was
so bored I got roped into helping
your mom feed the sea lions (by the
way, I'd be seriously worried about
your little sister cos I swear I saw
her eat a raw fish from the sea
lions' feed bucket).

You've been acting weird all week.
Whatever. I guess we're not best
friends any more.

Mark

Saturday April 11th

I woke up before it was light this morning and turned on my computer so I could keep researching werewolves. Now, more than ever, I need to find a way to cure the Were Virus. If I don't, then Professor Pickitt will show the world that everyone I care about grows a tail once a month!

I read for so long that my eyes stung. I read about the history of werewolves (there have been werewolf sightings as far back as ancient Rome), werewolf stories (there was a really nasty one where a princess was burned at the stake for being a werewolf), and werewolf breeds (there are four). But I learned nothing new about werewolf cures.

Then I remembered Dr. Lycan! In the madness of the last two days, I totally forgot to ask Donny about an address. Maybe I'd strike it lucky and find it on the Internet.

I quickly typed "Dr. Lycan" into the search engine and my stomach flipped like an excited eel when I saw what came up . . .

In 1983 a scientific paper was published by Dr. L. Lycan about the effects on a dog of drinking water infused with silver. After letting the silver sit in water under the light of the full moon, the potion was then fed to the dog. The effects were quite remarkable. The dog became quiet and calm and its fur began to molt.

Breakthrough!

Cut the cake and turn up the music—it's time to celebrate!

Cos Dr. Lycan was involved, I knew that when the paper talked about a "dog" it meant "werewolf."

I HAD to meet this crazy wolf doctor—now more than ever!

Desperate to share the news with Donny as soon as possible, I dressed and ran to the zoo at mega-speed.

Donny looked up from the pages of a battered old book as I burst into the Backstage offices. "Guess what?" I beamed proudly.

"What?" Donny asked, looking back down at his book; he didn't seem at all interested.

I quickly told him about the silver potion that Dr. Lycan had created.

There was a grunt from a corner of the room and I looked over and saw Red rolling her eyes as she picked a dusty book off Donny's bookshelf.

Emo Queen Red just makes zero sense to me.

The other day she was doing me a favor, telling me about Pickitt, and today she can't stand the sight of me. What's that about?

Donny studied me seriously and asked, "Did you ever hear back from that e-mail you sent Dr. Lycan?"

"Yes," I replied.

"And is it okay to go visit?" he asked.

"Yes," I lied, hoping that lie detection wasn't one of Red's freaky talents.

Donny sighed. "I can take you, but Sammy, don't get your hopes up. I've told you before that silver ingestion doesn't cure werewolves—"

"Look," I shouted, angry now, "you want to find out more about my CSC, right?" Donny nodded. "And I want to meet Dr. Lycan. If you drive me to Dr. Lycan's house, then I'll do anything you want—I promise."

Donny closed the book he was reading and I noticed the title on the cover: *Speaking to*

Animals. "Deal," he agreed. Red shook her head in disapproval, but clearly she knew better than to argue with Donny.

So that was it—the deal was made.

Donny had what he wanted and so did I.

Sunday April 12th

Today was a firm 9.5 on the Feral Scale of Weirdness.

Donny and Red came to pick me up in their van this morning. We drove for three hours to a small town called Hampton Mill to meet Dr. Lycan.

Red gave me the lowdown as Donny drove us down the highway. "Lycan was infected with the Were Virus as a child." She pulled out a grainy black-and-white photo of a young girl. The picture looked at least a hundred years old.

"Er, how old did you say she was?" I asked, trying to hide my shock that a) Dr. Lycan is a *she*, and b) she must have been born a couple of centuries ago!

Red ignored me and continued. "Her family disappeared around the same time. The assumption is that she killed them."

"There was never any proof of that," Donny chimed in, sounding slightly annoyed.

"Her werewolf genes have made her age slower than normal people," Red continued. "She's spent her whole life trying to find a cure for werewolfism."

"Without any success," Donny added.

Honestly, if either Donny or Red try to tell me one more time that there's no such thing as a werewolf cure, I might just trick them into the crocodile enclosure after dark!

Eventually Donny's van pulled up in front of a small, semidetached house. "We're here," he announced.

Before we'd even undone our seat belts, there was an old woman knocking on the car window. "What are you doing here, Donny?"

"Dr. Lycan!" Donny smiled, winding down the car window and reaching out. Dr. Lycan offered Donny a frail, wrinkled hand and gave him a grumpy smile.

"You're expecting us?" Donny said, getting out of the car.

Dr. Lycan's pale eyes locked onto me and I looked down sheepishly. "You're Sammy Feral," she said—as if she was accusing me of a terrible crime.

I held my breath, hoping she wasn't going to turn us away.

"You lied, didn't you?" Red said, guessing what was going on. "Dr. Lycan didn't tell you it was okay to visit, did she?"

Busted!

"Well, you're here now,"

Dr. Lycan grunted, pulling her cardigan tight around herself. "Come in. I'll make us some tea."

Phew! My high-risk plan had worked—we were in!

The inside of Dr. Lycan's house was like a museum. A museum of dogs. It stank of dogs and there were pictures of dogs on the walls, dog ornaments on the mantelpiece, dog collars

hanging from hooks on the walls, and worst of all, there were stuffed dogs everywhere. Spaniels, poodles, Great Danes, Labradors, German shepherds—you name the breed, Dr. Lycan had a stuffed one in her house.

YUCK x 1,000,000!!!!!!!!

We followed the doctor into her kitchen and she made us cups of tea. "I'm sorry," she apologized, opening the fridge and looking in, "I don't think I have anything in here that you'd like to eat. Unless I can tempt you to a chilled lung, or maybe an intestine fritter?"

"No, thank you," Donny said politely. "We've already eaten."

Donny might be polite, but he was a liar. We hadn't eaten, and I was starving. But I'd rather take a shower under an elephant with a stomach upset than eat anything from Dr. Lycan's fridge.

Anyway, we all sat down in the lounge (I tried really hard not to look at all the dead stuffed dogs everywhere) and began to talk.

"I don't normally let people visit," Dr. Lycan said carefully. "That's why I asked you not to come here." She gave me a sad smile and her eyes glazed over, as if she was remembering something. "I was your age when I was infected. I wish someone had been there to help me. And seeing you now, Sammy, I'm glad you came. Maybe I can help you, in a way that I always longed for someone to help me."

"You can help me find a cure." I beamed at her.

"I'm afraid there is no cure for people like me," Dr. Lycan said sadly. "I've spent all my life trying to discover one. I've tried everything: potions, lotions, meat starvation. You name it—I've tried it. None of it has worked."

"But what about your silver potion?" I asked, sounding slightly desperate. "I read about it on the Internet. You let it sit under the light of a full moon and then drank it. It made your fur fall out."

"Exactly." She grinned, shaking her head. "I lost my wolf fur—I wasn't cured, and the fur grew back."

I felt my throat tighten and the smile slipped from my face. I didn't want to believe Donny and Red when they said there was no such thing as a werewolf cure. But if Dr. Lycan had spent years trying—and failing—to find a cure, what made me think I could do it?

Dr. Lycan read the look of hopelessness on my face and her eyes filled up with tears. "Come with me," she said in a whisper.

She opened a door leading to a basement. For a split second I thought she was taking us down there to kill us and eat us . . . but thankfully that didn't happen.

The basement looked like the laboratory of a mad scientist. There were potions bubbling

away, strange flasks and jars filled with colorful things, a chalkboard with scientific equations written on it covering one whole wall, and in a corner of the room was a large cage. Inside the cage were straps and harnesses. "That's where I lock myself in," Dr. Lycan said. "Every month, when I feel the moon changing, I lock myself in with enough food and water to last three days. I haven't escaped, not once."

"And all of this," I pointed to the scientific experiments around the room, "has never helped cure you?"

"No." She shook her head. "But I'll keep trying, I won't give up. I write the results from my experiments in here." She walked over to a large leather-bound journal sitting on the side. "This is a record of how *not* to make a werewolf cure."

My heart sank to Dr. Lycan's basement floor. The journal was huge—she must have tried out hundreds of things, and none of them had worked.

"I'm getting old, Sammy," Dr. Lycan said quietly. "Even werewolves don't live forever. I've been thinking of passing this to someone." She picked up her heavy journal and held it to her chest. Then she held it out toward me. But there was fear in her eyes, like she'd get in major trouble if anyone knew she was handing me the journal. "Perhaps someone else can succeed where I have failed. Perhaps that could be you, Sammy."

Donny was just as shocked as I was. "Maybe I should take that," he said, reaching out for the journal.

Dr. Lycan snatched the heavy book back and held it close to her chest. "No, not you," she said. "Only Sammy. The only way this journal is leaving my house is in Sammy's hands."

"What do you want from Sammy in return?" Donny asked suspiciously.

"Nothing," she snapped at Donny. We all flinched slightly at her tone. She took a deep breath and forced a smile, "I just want to help you, Sammy. Maybe you'll have more luck than me."

Was Dr. Lycan insane? Of course—she was as crazy as a fish living in a tree house! Did I care?

Er, no! I had a scientific journal on werewolf experiments to read.

I took the journal with a grateful smile. "Thank you."

Looking down at the book, I suddenly felt a humongous wave of responsibility. Dr. Lycan had spent her whole life trying to find a werewolf cure—and now she was handing all her research over to me. I guess the least I can do is work as hard as possible to continue what she started. And the countdown is officially on—only 19 days until the next full moon.

"It's not right," I heard Donny whisper to Red on the way out. "Something's not right." He sounded suspicious.

No one said a thing on the way home. Donny drove in silence and Red buried her head in a book about Roman history. Seriously, Red has weird taste in books—why doesn't she read stuff about telekinesis instead of history textbooks?

I stared out of the car window, my mind buzzing with thoughts. I was hopeful, but also daunted by the task ahead. Finally I have something to get my teeth into . . . Dr. Lycan's journal might just be the key to helping me find a cure.

Monday April 13th

Think of the worst day you've ever had. Times that day by 10, step in a cowpie, let a bird poo on your head, and add a few school exams—that still wouldn't beat my day in the Bad Day Olympics!

Mark gave out invitations to his birthday party today. I didn't get one. He's not having it at the zoo any more. His parents have rented out the town hall instead. Tommy told me that there's gonna be a laser tag, Sumo wrestling suits, a barbecue, and paintball games in the back. And apparently it's a costume party—the theme is "Jungle Danger."

I can't believe Mark hasn't invited me—he knows I have the best snake costume in town.

But the worst thing that happened today . . . Pickitt came to the zoo again—and the pressure is ON!

Me, Dad, and Donny were in the Backstage offices when we heard a noise coming from the yard. We went out to investigate and there he was—the slimeball himself, his greasy hair slicked back and his shiny shoes trampling all over the zoo floor!

Pickitt held a tape measure up against the werewolf cage. "Do you think this cage would be big enough to hold a yeti?" he asked Dad with an evil smirk.

Dad's tired eyes flicked toward Donny for help.

"No, and even if it was," Donny replied, "this zoo is not for sale."

"I take it you haven't seen my legal notice

yet then?" Pickitt smirked, taking an envelope out of his jacket pocket and waving it about. The professor looked even more unhinged than on his last visit—his eyes crossed as he spoke and his tongue kept flicking out of his mouth like a lizard's. "I wasn't sure if you had, so I brought this along for you, Mr. Feral." Pickitt handed Dad a sealed envelope.

Dad opened the envelope and read. The color drained from his face and his hands shook. "Please," Dad choked on his words. "I'll do anything, please don't . . ."

Pickitt gave Dad a horrible oily grin and put his tape measure back in his pocket. "You have until the next full moon to be in touch."

And then he left. He just walked out as if nothing had happened.

"You've picked the wrong people to mess with, Pickitt," I shouted after him.

Then I lifted the letter out of Dad's trembling hands and read it aloud:

Dear Mr. Feral,

I no longer wish to buy Feral Zoo. You are going to give it to me instead.

If you don't, then I shall tell the world what you are. And once the world discovers that Feral Zoo is owned by a pack of werewolves, it won't take long before the Feral family is locked up and the zoo is closed down. You have until the next full moon.

Yours sincerely,

Professor P. Pickitt

It was as if the sky had clouded over and the world was about to end. How could this be happening? Dad and I looked at each other in horror—we were about to lose everything, for sure.

"It's okay," Dad said quietly, trying to hold it together.

But everything was far from okay.

"We'll find a way to stop him," Donny said confidently, seeing the shock on our faces. "He won't get away with this."

"Right about that," I agreed. "This is war!"

Tuesday April 14th

I was falling asleep in French this afternoon when my phone beeped in my pocket. It was a text from Donny:

Crisis meeting @ zoo 2nite

So right after school I headed over there. Mom caught me running near Darwin's cage and stopped me in my tracks by waving a broom covered in gorilla poo at me. "Er, Sammy, where do you think you're going?"

"Backstage," I replied. "Need to see Donny."

"The meeting's not till six," she said, brushing her frizzy hair from her face with the back of her hand. "Until then you have chores to do, please."

Er, since when was Mom invited? It's so annoying that you can never get anything past Mom—if Donny called a crisis meeting on the Moon, she'd probably find out about it.

"We'll all be there," Mom said, reading the confusion on my face. "I won't let the meeting start without you."

What could I say to that? I know better than to argue with Mom about zoo chores, especially when she's holding a poo-covered broom.

So I got to work. I helped Seb sweep out the otter enclosure. (Man, otters are surprisingly vicious! One nearly bit my thumb off today.)

Grace came to get me at five to six. "Hey, midget," she said in her most annoying big-sister voice, "time to head backstage." Honestly Mom might seem bossy—but Grace takes it to a whole new level. You can see where Natty gets it from!

Mom was right; everyone was in the Backstage offices: Donny, Red, Mom, Dad, Grace, even Natty, and even Caliban.

Donny stood on a chair and waved his hands until everyone was quiet. "Thanks for coming." He was wearing a bright purple T-shirt that made him look as pale as a ghost. "I asked everyone to come today because I want you to know that we're all in this together. This zoo has our protection," Donny added, and Red nodded in agreement. "And the reason why I called this meeting is that we have a plan."

My heart lifted like the flight of an eagle— Donny had a plan!

"We have to work together, as a team," he said, his eyes lighting up like a torch. "And everyone will have their role to play. This is what we're gonna do . . ."

Then he told us all what our jobs are until the next full moon. Check this out:

Donny and Red: Dig up as much dirt on Pickitt as possible—two can play the blackmail game!

Dad and Mom: Talk to the zoo's lawyer to make sure the deeds to the zoo are watertight.

Grace: Research other zoos that might be for sale—can't Pickitt buy one of those instead?

Natty: Throw people off the werewolf scent. Act "normally" so no one suspects that the Ferals are actually werewolves.

Me: Find a werewolf cure.

The fight is on!

The countdown has officially started. Seventeen days until the next full moon.

Wednesday April 15th
16 days to full moon

I'm in a race against time. If I don't find a cure for the Were Virus in the next 16 days, then I may as well pack my bags and ride away on Donny and Red's crazy train forever—cos there'll be nothing left for me here. No family, no friends, no zoo—no way, not an option, sorry!

This is my plan of action for the next 16 days:

* Start a potion—silver in water will be my first ingredient. Better than nothing.
* Read Dr. Lycan's journal and find clues for other possible potion ingredients.

* Brew a werewolf cure.

* Cure my family.

* Stop Pickitt from buying Feral Zoo.

* Catch up on homework—am in serious danger of flunking at the mo.

* Return to normal.

Dr. Lycan's journal has lists and lists of possible cures she's tried: antibiotics, blood transfusions, meat starvation, pickled eggs (I know, gross) . . . None of those things worked—so I won't waste my time with them. Instead I'm going to start by trying out anything that's NOT in Dr. Lycan's journal.

Only problem is, she's tried about a billion and one things, so thinking of something she hasn't tried is a bit like trying to get an elephant to walk a tightrope.

I was racking my brains on the way to school this morning. Mom and Natty were walking behind me. Natty goes to the elementary school next to mine and Mom takes her every day. They used to take Caliban too, but these days they don't want to risk him biting anyone so they leave him at home.

It's standard practice that I walk ahead. Natty's embarrassing at the best of times. But these days there's even more reason for me to avoid being seen in public with my little sister . . .

"But, Mom, I want raw sausages in my lunch box!" she screamed louder than a howler monkey.

"I told you," Mom whispered, trying to hush her. "No. We've all got to try to look normal."

Natty's never looked normal. Even when she wasn't a werewolf.

"But I want to eat meeeeeeeaaaat!" I heard Natty wail loudly. Mom was desperately shushing her but it wasn't working. Natty just started to scream louder and stomp her feet.

I was ready to tell her to stop being such a brat, but I had no words for what Natty did next.

My little sister broke free of Mom's grasp and ran, wailing and throwing her arms about, toward the duck pond. The ducks nervously flapped their wings and waddled off as Natty ran toward them. But one unsuspecting male mallard didn't budge—and Natty made a beeline straight for him.

I looked around in panic—terrified that the whole village was about to witness my sister tearing a live duck apart with her teeth. Unthinkable!

I began to chase after Natty, hoping I could stop her in time. Natty got to the water's edge and plunged in. She had begun to swim toward the duck when something stopped her.

Natty turned around and quick as a flash

pulled herself up out of the mucky water. She
looked down at her sodden school uniform; it
was covered with sloppy frog eggs.

Well, that's when Natty SERIOUSLY freaked
out!!

She started crying so loudly I thought my
eardrums would burst. Her wails sounded different
from before—she didn't sound angry, she sounded
scared.

Panic filled Mom's eyes as Natty tried to shake the frog eggs off her clothes and out of her hair. Mom mouthed the word, "No," and shook her head as if the world was about to end. She scooped Natty up in her arms and ran back toward home without a word of explanation.

Such drama, all cos Natty landed in a few frog eggs!

Natty slam-dunking in frogspawn ranks a healthy 6 on the Feral Scale of Weirdness.

Conclusion = frog eggs and werewolves do not mix well.

I've cross-referenced Dr. Lycan's journal, and frogspawn is not something she's tried.

I doubt frog eggs alone could cure werewolves . . . but as part of a potion . . . maybe?

Potion ingredient number 2 = frog eggs.

Thursday April 16th
15 days to full moon

Today was the day I started brewing my very own werewolf cure!

I made it to the zoo after school and headed straight for the Backstage offices. "Can you help me with something?" I asked Donny, who was busy cleaning up leftover ashes from his pet phoenix, who'd burst into flames this morning.

"Not a good time," Donny replied, handing a bag of ashes to Red. "I'm about to go out. There's been an urban yeti sighting a few towns away. I need to go and investigate." Donny threw me a thoughtful look, "You and I still need to have a serious chat about your CSC . . ."

"That's not why I needed to see you," I said, feeling annoyed.

I wish Donny would drop the whole CSC thing and focus on what's important—like brewing my potion!

"Whatever you need"—Donny pushed his gray hair from his eyes—"Red can help you."

Red let out a groan like a demented seal as she swung the bag of phoenix ashes into the garbage can. She seemed to be in one of her moods. I can't work out if she puts it on to match her makeup or if she really is as miserable as a molting manatee.

Red yawned as I told her how silver and frog eggs are the first two ingredients in my potion. "So I just need some help collecting frog eggs," I finished.

"Lead the way," Red said reluctantly.

Feral Zoo has 50 species of frog living in the amphibian house. That might sound like loads, but considering there are over 3,500 frog species in the world, it's not a lot at all.

Red scared away the zoo visitors while I quickly collected a jar of fresh frogspawn.

After I'd locked the frog tank back up, we headed Backstage.

"Where does Donny keep his silver darts?" I asked, looking around. Red pointed to a large sack lying next to Donny's camp bed. "Hopefully he won't mind me borrowing a couple of these bad boys," I muttered, taking a few from the bag.

I added the silver darts to the jar of frog eggs, screwed the lid back on, and placed the jar inside an empty kitchen cupboard.

*

"That," I said proudly, looking at the jar, "is the beginnings of my potion!"

Red snickered. "Like you know what you're doing!"

Friday April 17th
14 days to full moon

I spent today reading Dr. Lycan's journal at every opportunity: walking to school, on my lunch break, on the toilet, over dinner, and in bed.

I've never read so much in my life! My eyes are so tired I'm gonna need matchsticks to hold them open if I'm awake for much longer. So I'm going to bed. Will write more tomorrow—promise.

Saturday April 18th
13 days to full moon

Today is Mark's birthday party. Practically the entire school was invited apart from me. Normally, I'd be mega-bummed about stuff like that, but right now I've got bigger things to worry about . . . ingredients for my potion!

Every second I'm awake is being dedicated to perfecting the brew. As well as being a webaholic, I've also become a journal-obsessed bookworm. I just can't get enough of Dr. Lycan's journal!

Check out this passage I read as I ate my toast this morning:

There's something about eagle feathers that I can't put my finger on. When I hold them I seem to lose my werewolf sense of smell. Yet they don't cure me. I've been investigating their molecular structure and . . .

My phone beeped. I stopped reading. It was a text from Donny.

Fancy a day of CSC experiments?

A day of CSC experiments = not exactly how I wanna spend my day. Give me research into eagle feathers, please! But I *had* promised Donny I'd help him with his CSC research if he took me to see Dr. Lycan.

Donny's idea of CSC experiments involved me just speaking to his pets. Honestly, I was kinda relieved—I'd been psyching myself up for blood tests and X-rays!

Donny watched me carefully and took notes. His notebook already looks half used—I guess he's been writing notes about me ever since he arrived!

I spent ages talking to all three heads of Donny's gut worm, the fire-breathing turtle, and the phoenix. As the hours went by I got seriously restless. "With all due crypto-respect, Donny," I huffed, "can't we do this after we've dealt with Pickitt?"

Donny snapped his notebook shut. "Sure."

Well, that was easy!

I gave him a quick lowdown on Dr. Lycan's

journal and everything she'd tried that hadn't worked.

"I just don't understand why she's given you her journal." Donny frowned. "I've known Dr. Lycan for a long time, she doesn't ever help anyone."

"That's not the point," I said. "The point is that this journal is the key to finding ingredients for my potion. I read this really interesting passage this morning. Here . . ." I took out the journal from my bag, found the passage about eagle feathers, and handed it to Donny.

He read quickly. "Interesting. It reminds me of a remote werewolf community that lived in the Himalayas hundreds of years ago . . ."

He dropped Dr. Lycan's journal and went over to his bookshelf. He scanned the shelves until he found what he was looking for. The book looked ancient; the pages were thin and the print was tiny. As Donny brought the book over I realized that it was written in another language.

"Just as I thought," Donny mumbled, and then he read from the book, translating as he spoke: "'The pack bred eagles and the birds lived among them. The pack's alpha claimed that the eagles held a mystical power that allowed the wolves to regain many of their human traits . . .'"

Bingo!

"Oh man." I smiled. "Gotta add some eagle feathers to my potion!"

There are advantages to having your own family zoo. I ran into the main area, past Darwin's cage, past the polar bears, and past the reptile house. I arrived at the aviaries. Zoo visitors watched as I let myself into Eddie the eagle's cage and collected some of his old feathers from the ground.

A mega-strange thing happened when I added

Eddie's feathers to the frogspawn and silver . . .
they let off purple smoke . . . I'd register it as a
solid 4 on the Feral Scale of Weirdness.

Potion ingredient number 3 = eagle feathers.

Sunday April 19th
12 days to full moon

I had a majorly mysterious e-mail from Dr. Lycan today. Check this out:

Sammy,

I do hope my journal is helping you. It's the least I could do for you after what I've done to your family. I'm so, so sorry.

Dr. L. Lycan

Er, major confuzzlement. What does she have to be sorry about?

If it wasn't for Dr. Lycan's journal, I'd still be relying on useless Internet sites that tell werewolves to kneel in the same spot for 100 years!

I'd say Dr. Lycan's e-mail on Feral Scale of Weirdness = 5.

Monday April 20th
11 days to full moon

I got 8% in my biology test today.

Mrs. Brown made me stay behind after class. "Is everything okay at home, Sammy?" she said softly, her head tilted to one side.

"Sure." I shrugged. My legs started to twitch like a grasshopper; I just wanted to run away. The last thing I need in my life right now is a nosy teacher!

"It's just . . . I've noticed that you seem very quiet recently. You don't seem to be spending time with your friends, and your grades have dropped." I didn't say anything. I was as silent as a tiger out hunting. Mrs. Brown's forehead creased into a worried frown. "I think the best thing for you would be to stay behind after school, until you've caught up with all the work you're behind on."

Er, staying behind after school = detention!

Nothing in the world can be worse than detention when I have 11 days to find a werewolf cure.

"Mrs. Brown," I tried reasoning with her, "I can't stay behind. You see—"

"You'll report to me after school every day this week, Sammy," she said sternly. "No excuses."

Mrs. Brown = evil incarnate!

If only she knew how much of a disaster zone my life was at the moment! If only I'd studied for my stupid biology test! If only there was no such thing as detention!

WHAT AM I GOING TO DO???

This is totally crudtacular!

With 11 days to find a cure I have only three lousy ingredients in my potion jar.

I need to step up my game. I need to be more focused. I need to stay up all night reading Dr. Lycan's journal. I need more clues!

Tuesday April 21st
10 days to full moon

After school today I showed up at detention.

Mrs. Brown told me to study the life cycle of a tapeworm, but I had other ideas.

I tucked Dr. Lycan's journal in between the pages of my science textbook and read that instead.

Clever? I thought so . . .

I was so engrossed in the journal (reading about a time Dr. Lycan tried eating caterpillars and her ear hair turned blue), that I didn't notice Mrs. Brown standing behind me, peering over my shoulder.

Mrs. Brown looking over my shoulder = bad news!

"What's that?" she asked, her voice sounding controlled, but I could hear rage bubbling away underneath.

I slammed my textbook shut. "Nothing."

Mrs. Brown took the biology book from my hands, shook it open, and pulled out Dr. Lycan's journal.

She studied it for a moment as the veins in the side of her temple pulsed to an angry beat. "This, Sammy Feral," she said, through gritted teeth, "is utterly unacceptable. You need to understand the importance of education!"

Er, no, you need to understand the importance of keeping your nose out of other people's business!

"Don't think you'll be seeing this"—she waved Dr. Lycan's journal in my face—"again until the end of term." She tutted impatiently.

"Honestly, children today . . ." she muttered to herself in disgust.

Then she stormed off, the journal in her hands.

Panic! Help! SOS!

Dr. Lycan's journal is my guide to finding a cure. Without it I'm as stuffed as the dogs in Dr. Lycan's living room.

What am I going to do now?

Arrrrgggghhhhh!!!!!

Saturday April 25th
6 days to full moon

There's a reason I haven't written in my diary for four days—I've been spending every minute of every hour researching possible ingredients for my potion. Without Dr. Lycan's journal.

There's been no time for diary writing. There's been no time for anything—last night Mom found out I hadn't brushed my teeth since Wednesday. "Sammy, your breath smells worse than the back end of a rhino!" she complained.

Er, sorry, no time for personal hygiene—I'm trying to save your furry backside!

Has there been potion progress these last few days? I'm pleased to report that, yes, there has.

I now have five ingredients:

1	Silver water
2	Frogspawn
3	Eagle feathers
4	Grace's hair
5	Anaconda skin

The idea for the hair came to me in biology class. I was listening to Mrs. Brown droning on when for once she said something interesting . . .

"Did you know, class, that when you're immunized against a disease, what actually happens is that you're injected with a very small amount of that disease? Your immune system begins to build up a special defense to it—so whenever you come into contact with it again, you can fight it off."

That's when an idea popped into my head.

Maybe adding werewolf DNA to my potion would be a good idea.

I pitched the idea to everyone over dinner that night, and that's when Grace agreed to give me her ear-hair clippings.

Result!

The idea for the anaconda skin came to me when I was at the zoo last night.

I got to the zoo to find Dad, Seb, and Max all standing by Clint the crocodile's enclosure and talking about mating him with a girl crocodile called Wendy.

I stuck around and listened for a while—I like learning stuff about crocodiles; crocodiles are really cool. Did you know that crocodiles have been around since the dinosaurs? Anyway, soon the conversation turned to general animal mating, and I got bored.

"I'm gonna head Backstage and see Donny," I told Dad.

"The anacondas could do with their monthly feeding," Dad said. Then he bent down and whispered so only I could hear, "I can't go near them for some reason. Neither can your Mom or sisters. I think it must be a you-know-what thing."

Werewolves are scared of anacondas? Hmm, a definite 4 on the Feral Scale of Weirdness, I'd say.

So I headed to the reptile house and took out a load of frozen mice from the freezer. I took my time with each snake, watching them dislocate their jaw and gobble the mouse down in one. I never get bored of that—it's so cool.

When I got to Andy's tank (he's one of the biggest anacondas) I spotted that he'd shed his skin.

An idea hit me like a swipe from a tiger's paw: if werewolves had a fear of anacondas, maybe anaconda skin would be a good ingredient for my potion!

While Andy was busy swallowing a frozen mouse, I opened the tank lid and carefully reached in and picked up his skin. Snakeskin feels kind of dry and crispy, even though it looks wet and slimy—so you have to be careful with it.

I added the snakeskin to the jar of other ingredients in the Backstage kitchen cupboard and gave it a good shake.

Here's a quick update on everything else that's gone on over the last few days:

* Donny watched me have a conversation with Nim, his fire-breathing turtle. Nim told me all about the jungle swamps of Borneo.
* Red discovered that Professor Pickitt and Dr. Lycan once worked at the same science laboratory.

* Grace and Max had an argument cos Grace hardly spends any time with him these days.

* Natty's going around the zoo like she owns the place, telling everyone what to do in case we "give ourselves away."

* Mark brought his party photos into school and everyone wouldn't shut up about what a great party it was.

Will try to write again tomorrow. I won't leave it so long next time.

Sunday April 26th
5 days to full moon

One thing I will say about Red is that she always keeps herself busy. When she's not helping Donny, she's reading. And when she's not reading, she's practicing her powers—today I found her Backstage tying metal forks into knots.

"Donny's not here," she informed me, without looking up from the fork in her hand. She didn't say where he was—she probably didn't even know. Donny's such a mystery, it wouldn't surprise me if Red knew as little about him as I did.

"Oh," I said, slumping into a chair by the

phoenix's cage. Since hatching the other day the bird was now the size of a small chick. He cocked his head to one side and stared at me. I waited to see if he'd say anything, but he didn't.

"You okay, kid?" Red asked, putting down the fork and picking up a book about art history.

"My family are still werewolves," I answered. "I've had better days." Red snorted and opened up the book. "Why are you always reading school books?" I asked. "Why don't you just go to school?"

"Donny's never been to school," Red muttered. "He turned out okay."

Man, how come they get out of going to school and I don't?

I looked over at the fork Red had tied into a knot. "When did you first know you could do it?" I blurted out. "You know—move things with your mind."

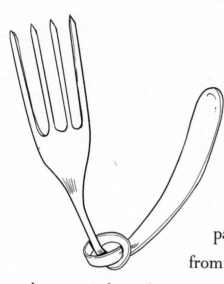

Red looked me right in the eye, "You really wanna know?" she asked. I nodded. "When I was small." She closed the art book. "I never knew my parents. I was passed from one kids' home to the next. I always knew I was different. If I wanted a toy, all I had to do was will it to come to me and it did. My powers freaked people out. No one wanted to adopt me.

"I met Donny when I was 13. He was in town investigating mothman sightings. The next day I packed my bags and ran away with him. He made me realize that I didn't have to be alone."

Red's story made me think. I found it tough when my parents weren't around for three days at the last full moon. I can't imagine what it would be like if they'd never, ever been around. Maybe I'd been hard on Red. Maybe I'd be as prickly as a porcupine too if I'd had her life.

"Mind if I hang out here today?" I asked her, trying to be friendly.

"Be my guest, kid," she replied, standing up. "I'm heading out—gonna hit Pickitt's house and see what I can find there."

"You're gonna break in and snoop?" I asked, alarmed. I might let Red off the hook for a being moody goth, but not for being a burglar!

"Chill, kid." She laughed. "It's amazing what kind of stuff can float out through an open window."

So Red headed out and left me alone in the Backstage offices.

I was BORED! The zoo wasn't busy, Mark wasn't speaking to me, and Donny and Red had gone out. What was I supposed to do? Help Natty

to clean out the guinea-pig runs?
Er, no, thanks—I'd rather
cuddle a gut worm!

What I really
wanted to do
was work on my
werewolf cure—
but Mrs. Brown
still had Dr. Lycan's
journal. I stared out
of the window into the
Backstage yard, thinking
about what I could do . . .

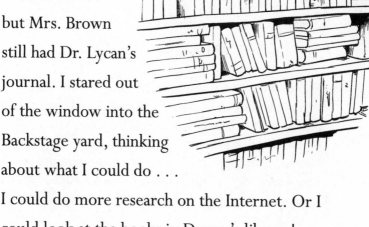

I could do more research on the Internet. Or I
could look at the books in Donny's library!

Bingo!

I didn't bother counting them, but Donny has
way over 1,000 books. I spent ages scanning the
shelves, picking out any books on werewolves that
were written in English.

Beasts of the Moon

The History of Were

The Werewolf Within

I read, read, read for hours—until my eyes stung. I read about the history of werewolves, how the Were Virus affects different animals, and how werewolves react to different elements.

And then I read this:

> There was a reported outbreak of the Were Virus in eastern Russia in the early fifteenth century. The beasts were subdued by forcing them to drink quicksilver. Quicksilver, of course, is highly toxic to most living creatures. However, once administered to werewolves, it reduces aggression and restores normal human characteristics.

What was quicksilver? I'd never heard of it before. Was it just a type of silver? Cos I already had silver shards in my potion.

Quicksilver = my new obsession.

I have to find a way to get some!

I took out my phone and texted Donny:

> What's quicksilver? I need
> sum 4 my potion.

He still hasn't texted me back.

2 A.M.

It's the middle of the night and I've just been woken by a text from Donny.

> Quicksilver is another
> name 4 mercury.

Monday April 27th
4 days to full moon

Today was gnarlier than a hyena singing a love song.

I found out what Dr. Lycan meant in her e-mail when she said she was sorry.

It's bad. It's really, really bad.

"I found this in Professor Pickitt's e-mail account," Red said, waving a printed e-mail at me.

"Since when did printing out Professor Pickitt's e-mails involve levitating stuff through windows?" I asked. I knew Red was lying when she said she wasn't gonna break into Pickitt's house.

"Sammy, you should read the e-mail," Donny said seriously. "It explains why Dr. Lycan was so keen to give you her journal—she was feeling guilty."

Monday April 6th,

To Professor Pickitt,

You've always been very kind to me, funding my research. And you've never asked for much in return—all you want is information, if I should have any.

Well, I have some very interesting information for you. Information that I hope you'll agree will cost you at least another year's funding for my were-cure project.

A family has been turned into werewolves. They're called the Ferals and they own a zoo. The father, mother and two daughters were infected. However there's a son, called Sammy, who is still healthy.

I look forward to hearing from you.

Many thanks,

Dr. L. Lycan

"She must have sent it as soon as I first e-mailed her!" I muttered, in shock from what I'd read. "How could she do this? It's all her fault."

"It's my fault, Sammy," Donny said quietly. "I should have known she couldn't be trusted. I'm sorry."

I shook my head in disbelief. "It's not your fault," I told Donny. "You didn't know. And besides, if we hadn't visited her then I'd never have had a chance to read through her journal. At least this way I didn't waste my time putting sour milk, dust, or fish scales into my potion. Dr. Lycan got there first."

I tried not to feel bummed about Dr. Lycan's e-mail, but the truth is that I've never felt so betrayed in all my life. Basically, today sucked worse than rotten duck eggs!

The only thing that can save us—save the zoo and save me from living on the streets with nothing but pigeons for friends—is finding a cure for the Were Virus. I'm trying hard to do that, but clearly I need to try harder, and from now on I'm going to be mega-careful who I trust!

Tuesday April 28th
3 days to full moon

Got this text from Donny today:

> Am hatching a plan
> to get quicksilver

No idea what Donny's plan involves, but I'd try anything right now. Only three days until the full moon, until my family turns into werewolves again, until Pickitt takes the zoo away from us, and life as I know it is over . . .

Wednesday April 29th
2 days to full moon

I was planning to write all about what happened at school today (Tommy accidentally set fire to the science lab and Katrina's pencil case went up in flames), but something way more important has just happened . . .

I came back from school today to find that Dad was still at the zoo and Mom was cooking spaghetti bolognese. She was making loads, which is unusual these days as I'm the only one who eats normal food.

"Why are you cooking so much?" I asked her.

"Max is here," she told me, pinching her nose

in disgust at the smell of the bolognese sauce. "He's joining us for dinner. He's in the living room with Grace now."

No way did I want to witness Grace and Max's smooch-fest so I went upstairs to my room.

I opened my bedroom door to find Natty (aka Annoying Brat Supreme) in my room, reading my diary.

"What are you doing, squirt?" I shouted, lunging toward her and snatching the notebook. "You know you're banned from my room—the last time I found you in here you stole a load of my dinosaur books to make a run for Harry. They still stink of hamster pee!"

"Why are you writing about me?" she asked.

"Like you can even read," I said.

"I can read, actually," she shouted back. "I'm very good at reading. I'm the best in my class."

"That doesn't give you the right to go through my stuff!" I yelled.

Natty snarled and clenched her fists. I could tell she was about to go all wolfy on me so I stepped back, ready to defend myself.

Natty's lips began to quiver and pull back around her clenched teeth.

My feet were inching away from her—no way did I want to end up like Harry—when a piercing scream came from downstairs.

It took me a few seconds to realize that there were actually two people screaming, not just one. It sounded like Grace and Max.

I ran downstairs, with Natty following close behind.

Max was lying on the living-room floor

clutching his neck. There was blood pouring through his hands.

"She bit me," he said, his eyes like a frightened horse's. "We were . . . you know . . . and she bit me." Max was pointing at Grace, who was just standing there, staring at him in shock.

"I don't know what came over me . . ." she whispered, her face as white as a polar-bear den. "I just . . . I just . . . I wanted him to understand. Oh, what have I done?"

Caliban was wagging his tail in delight. He started howling loudly.

Take him out," Mom instructed Natty. "We need some space."

Natty grabbed Caliban's collar and pulled him into the hallway. They stood just outside the living room, watching what was going on.

"Sammy, get a bowl of water and a clean towel," Mom instructed. "We need to wash out the wound."

"It's too late," Grace whispered.

"No, it's not," Mom shouted. The panic in her voice was scaring me.

"What have you done?" Max whispered at Grace.

Grace began to cry. "I wanted to tell you . . . But I thought you'd dump me if you knew."

"Tell me what?" he asked.

"Grace, that's enough!" Mom warned. "Sammy—water! NOW!"

I ran out of the room and headed to the

kitchen, where I filled a plastic tub with warm water and took a clean dish towel from under the sink.

When I got back to the living room Grace was kneeling over Max and sobbing, "I'm sorry, I'm so sorry . . ."

We never did get to eat the bolognese. It went cold, and all I had for dinner was toast.

After all the fuss had died down and Max's wound had been cleaned, Mom asked him if he was hungry and he replied, "I've got a real craving for raw sausages. Do you have any?"

That basically confirms the worst—when the full moon comes around I'll have six werewolves to deal with instead of five: Mom, Dad, Grace, Natty, Caliban, and Max.

Thursday April 30th
1 day to full moon

Until today, the worst thing I'd ever done was accidentally kill a frog by keeping it in my pocket for too long. But this evening I'm planning to break into my school and steal mercury from the chemistry lab . . . and that's a bazillion times worse than accidental frog murder.

It all started in chemistry today. We had a test on fossil fuels, and we were all split up so we couldn't copy each other's answers. I had to sit in front of the glass cabinet where the chemicals used for experiments are kept. That's when I spotted the mercury.

Then I remembered the text that Donny had sent me in the middle of the night: "Quicksilver is another name 4 mercury."

Newsflash: I need to add mercury to my potion!

I hung around the chemistry lab at break and lunchtime today. Honestly, you'd think the chemicals cabinets were stacked with diamonds the size of my head—they were guarded at all times! There was zero chance I could get my hands on mercury during school hours.

So this is my plan:

* Meet up with Donny and Red tonight.
* Sneak into school under the cover of darkness.
* Go to the chemistry lab, open the cabinet, and steal the mercury.
* Add mercury to my potion.

9:30 P.M.

The pressure's on—BIG TIME. We've only got one shot to get this right. The full moon is tomorrow. There's no time for mistakes or second chances.

My parents would flip more than a salmon rushing upstream if they knew what I was planning. So I was extra well behaved this evening to keep them off the scent. I came back from school, did my homework, ate dinner, and even helped Natty with her spelling.

Right now it's dark outside and everyone's gone to bed.

I'm about to sneak out of the house by climbing through my window and down the drainpipe.

I'm gonna need all the luck in the world to pull this off.

Will write later . . .

MIDNIGHT

I have never, ever done anything so bad in all my life. I want to be a zookeeper when I grow up—not a criminal!

I snuck out of the house and met Donny and Red, who were waiting for me at the zoo. They were both dressed head to toe in black. Donny was so pale he looked like a ghoul in his black gear!

"So, do we just sneak in?" I asked, clinging to the shadows as we walked. Even at that stage—

before we'd gotten to school—I was afraid the cops were after us. I kept checking over my shoulder every two seconds, like an owl with a neck twitch!

"Chill, kid," Red whispered. The night was cold and her breath clung to the air in small white puffs as she spoke. "I'm an old hand at this kind of stuff. You can go back to bed if you want; leave it to me."

I chewed the inside of my mouth. Considering her skinny hips, narrow shoulders, and lack of social conscience, I had no doubt that Red would make a world-class burglar. And sure, of course it was tempting to let her do my dirty work—but this was my idea, and my potion. If anyone was taking risks and leading the way, it had to be me.

"We're in this together," I said. "And if it all goes wrong, I'll take the rap. It was my idea."

I glanced across to Donny and Red, who both nodded.

We walked the rest of the way in silence. I ran the plan over in my head, like a song on repeat. I knew what to do—but what if it all went wrong? We could get arrested! Who would find a cure and save the zoo if Donny, Red, and I were all locked up in jail?

I pushed those thoughts to the back of my mind and tried to stay focused.

My school is surrounded by tall metal fencing, with sharp barbed wire at the top. Most criminals would have to scramble over the top—but not us, not when Red was around.

She stared hard at the metal fence and it soon began to creak and bend.

"Can't you be a bit quieter when you do that?" I hissed.

She turned her head and gave me a look that could turn a speeding cheetah to stone. "I guess that's a no," I muttered.

Before long there was a gap in the fence wide enough to climb through.

"Over to you, Sammy," Red instructed.

Deep breath . . . this was it . . . we were going in . . .

I led the way through the school playground, being careful to keep to the shadows so the security cameras didn't catch us.

There were four main entrances to my school: the main entrance at the front, the entrance to the high school wing, and two fire exits. I decided the high school entrance would be best, cos it was nearest to the chemistry lab.

We reached the entrance and I gave the instructions: "Right, once we're in the high school wing we need to head to the corridor, turn right, take a left, then the lab is third on the right. As soon as we have the mercury, we make a run for it, okay?"

"If we get split up, then we meet back at the zoo," Donny said.

"Understood," Red agreed, pulling a balaclava over her face—she was wearing extra black makeup for the occasion.

It was showtime!

My heart was thumping like a herd of wildebeests—I'd never been so terrified in all my life.

I took a deep breath and gave Red a thumbs-up. "Time to rock 'n' roll."

My ears rung with the sound of shattering

glass as Red blasted the door open—I hadn't realized she was going to destroy it!

Before I could complain a blaring alarm rang through my skull. We'd set off the school alarm—and it was LOUD! We only had minutes before the cops arrived. The alarm would be wired to the nearest police station for sure!

My stomach flipped around inside me like a lake full of hungry eels as I raced through the high school wing.

But before we'd even made it to the main corridor, a voice came booming out from somewhere . . .

"Who's there? The police are on their way!"

WHAT??? NO!!!

The sound of a dog frantically barking echoed through the school. It sounded like a big dog—a German shepherd or a Doberman. A guard dog!

A tight, airless feeling gripped my chest and I couldn't breathe.

"A security guard?" Donny sounded panicked. "You didn't mention a security guard!"

"I didn't know there was one!" My heart felt as if it was going to explode in my chest, it was beating so fast. Security guards and guard dogs were NOT part of my plan!

"We've come this far," Red said fearlessly. "We can't run away. Sammy, lead the way."

Without thinking, my feet carried me around the corner. There was a gray-haired security guard standing at the end of the corridor, with a large dog on a leash.

I ran as fast as I could in the opposite direction, and Donny and Red followed. The speeding footsteps of the guard and his dog chased after us.

"Shut the fire doors behind you!" I shouted as we bolted through the halls. Red slammed the fire doors shut behind her. The heavy doors stopped the yapping dog in his tracks. Result!

But the mission was far from over . . .

We arrived at the chemistry lab. The door was locked. Red blasted it open in seconds. I ran over to the cabinet—my hands were shaking like crazy but I managed to steady them. The cabinet door swung open and I lifted the mercury off the shelf.

It was in my hands—I had the missing ingredient for my potion in my grasp!

But there was no time for celebration.

The sound of police sirens filled the air.

We had to get out of there—fast!

"No time for doors!" Donny shouted. "We're taking the window!"

I pushed open a window and climbed through. I spotted police cars pulling up by the main entrance. They were after us!

My heart pounded like an army of gorillas beating their chests. This was it—I was going to be locked up in jail and the key would be thrown into a swamp full of alligators. I was busted!

No way could I let that happen. I had to get away!

I don't even remember if Donny and Red were by my side. All I remember is running away so fast I thought my legs were gonna fall off. I probably smashed world records with the speed I was going!

Donny and Red met me at the zoo gates— like we planned. We headed Backstage so I could add the mercury to my potion, then I left to go home.

All the way home I couldn't stop looking over my shoulder—I kept expecting to see guards or the police or even the army coming after me!

I promise on Beelzebub's life that I will never,

ever do anything so bad ever again. I only did it because I didn't have a choice.

The full moon starts tomorrow—TOMORROW!!

And the fate of the zoo depends on me, and tonight I proved that I'd do anything to save it!

Friday May 1st

The full moon starts tonight.

BANG, BANG, BANG!

There was a loud banging on our front door early this morning. I was still in bed. My heart froze in my chest—I was sure it was the police coming to arrest me.

Then I heard Mom and Dad's bedroom door swing open and someone rush down the stairs. I flew out of bed quicker than a hawk swooping on prey—I had to stop them from answering the door!

"Mr. Feral, Mrs. Feral?" a woman shouted through the mail slot.

I grabbed hold of Dad's pajama sleeve as he reached for the front door. "Dad, no," I pleaded. But he opened the door anyway.

It wasn't the police. It wasn't my principal. It wasn't the army. It wasn't what I was expecting . . .

A flashbulb went off in Dad's face and a woman holding a tape recorder bullied her way through the front door. "My name's Brenda, I'm a reporter. I've come here to interview the owners of Feral Zoo."

"Excuse me?" Dad asked, rubbing sleep from his eyes.

I could have cried with relief. It was just a reporter, probably coming to see if we were running for Zoo of the Year again.

"Are you Mr. Feral?" the woman asked with a sparkle in her eye. She leaned in and spoke quietly. "I know all about your condition, Mr. Feral. You're a werewolf, and so are your wife and daughters. I can get you the best newspaper deal around. I could make you very rich."

"I don't know what you're talking about," Dad snapped, pushing the woman out of the door. "If you bother me or my family again, I'll call the police." He slammed the door in her face.

Er, rewind—a reporter knows about Dad being a werewolf? About Mom and the girls being werewolves?!!

"Three guesses who invited her here." Dad sighed.

I didn't need three guesses—I knew right away: Professor Pickitt.

So that was Pickitt's plan? He was gonna tip off every journalist in the country and let them see for themselves what happens when the sun sets this evening.

That guy is sneakier than a fox in a chicken farm!

"What did that lady want?" Natty called down to us. Mom scooped Natty up and brought her downstairs. Grace followed behind, yawning. "Shouldn't I be trotting around on all fours by now?" she asked, scratching her messy morning hair.

"Not until it gets dark this evening," I said. "And werewolves don't trot. You should know that."

Bad idea to argue with Grace first thing in the morning—especially when the moon's about to turn. She clenched her fists and opened her mouth to shout, but thankfully Dad cut her off.

"We need to get to the zoo—now," he said. Then he filled them in on what the reporter knew.

Mom twitched the lace curtains by the front

door and peered out. "We've got serious trouble."

"Look, we've done everything we can," Dad said with a deep sigh. "The best thing we can do now is just head to the zoo and let Donny lock us up."

"There's always my potion," I said hopefully. "I've got a good feeling about it, and—"

"Sammy, everyone knows there's no such thing as a werewolf cure," Grace shouted. I could see tears welling up in her eyes. "Whatever stupid science experiment you've got going on isn't gonna work. The only reason Donny let you carry on with it was to shut you up and keep you busy!"

"That's not true!" I shouted back, feeling angry. "If that was true, then why would he bother helping me?"

"You're so stupid!" Grace shrieked. Full-on tears were streaming down her face now. "Our lives are ruined. And you're too busy messing around with nose-hair clippings and frogspawn to even . . . to even . . ."

Mom put her arms around Grace, who sobbed hysterically into Mom's bathrobe. Then Natty started crying too. I looked over at Dad—he's usually good at sticking up for me when the girls gang up on me.

But Dad just shrugged. "I think you should go and get dressed, Sammy."

What? Did everyone think my potion was a waste of time? I clenched my teeth to stop myself from screaming—if only everyone knew what I'd risked to make that potion, then maybe they'd be a bit more grateful!

I stormed upstairs and got dressed. As soon as everyone was ready Dad barged past the reporters standing in the front garden (there were about 30 of them by now) and bundled us all into the car.

Grace's whimpering provided the soundtrack for our drive to the zoo. I don't think I've ever seen her so upset—she didn't even cry that much the time I told the whole school she had lice!

"What about school?" I asked Mom, as we got out of the car.

"School . . . oh . . . right . . ." Mom sounded really flustered. "Look, Sammy, I'd just rather you stayed close by. Don't worry about school." Being so near to the full moon was making Mom C.R.A.Z.Y.—she'd never usually let me skip school.

3 P.M.

We all went Backstage as soon as we arrived at the zoo. And I went straight to get my potion.

"Well, it's as good as it's going to get," I muttered, shaking the jar.

"It's looking good," Red said, leaning over my shoulder to inspect the potion. That was the nearest thing to a compliment I'd ever had from her. I allowed myself a little smile. "Are you going to give it to them right away?" she asked.

"I think it needs to brew a bit longer first," I said, watching the mercury fizzle around inside the jar.

"It would probably be a good idea to let it brew under the light of a full moon," Donny suggested casually, as if he's made a million werewolf cures before.

Half an hour later Max arrived at the Backstage gate. He looked as scared as a bat in a bubble bath. I don't blame the guy—I've seen people turn into werewolves before and it ain't pretty!

Max and Grace spent the next couple of hours just hugging and crying. Seriously, I feel bad that she's a werewolf and all, but Grace is really annoying me today. All she's done so far is cry—how's that gonna help anyone?

The morning passed in a bit of a haze. Once

Donny had assured me that the government probably hadn't issued "Most Wanted" posters with my face on them, I tried to distract myself from what's gonna happen when the sun sets. I even swept out Nim's smelly turtle tank and read a chapter of Red's math textbook.

Desperation Supreme!

Around lunchtime Dad, Mom, Grace, Natty, Max, and Caliban came into the Backstage offices. They looked like they'd just had a meeting about something.

"We've decided that we should be locked up now," Dad said seriously to Donny. "We don't want to take any risks."

"I agree," said Donny.

My parents, sisters, and Max all held hands as Donny led them into the cage. Caliban obediently stayed by Dad's side as the cage door clanged shut.

"Sammy," Mom said, calling me over. She

reached her hands through the bars. I let Mom take my hands in hers. "Whatever happens, remember we all love you very much."

"I know," I said, trying to sound brave. Dread was starting to creep through me—I only had a few hours left before all the people I cared about turned into killers. "Don't worry about the zoo," I said. "We'll protect it. I'll see you in a few days' time."

6:30 P.M.

It's getting dark outside. I feel sick—so sick I think I could puke my guts out until there's nothing left inside me. Memories of last month's full moon make me wanna scream. I wish I could just freeze time. I wish the moon would never be full again.

Time to witness Werewolf Family, take two. Great.

I'm gonna take Donny's advice and let my potion brew under the light of a full moon. I don't wanna mess this up—and if I trust anyone when it comes to werewolf advice, it's Donny. He's been right about everything else so far.

As soon as the sun rises tomorrow I'm going to feed my potion to the werewolves and see what happens . . .

Saturday May 2nd

Before this morning, the worst thing I'd ever opened my eyes to see was Natty pooping on my bedroom carpet (she was pretty tiny at the time).

But what I woke up and saw this morning was way, way worse . . .

As the sun set last night, the full moon rose into the sky. It looked like there was a ring of blood around it—kind of fitting when you considered what was about to go down at Feral Zoo . . .

Everyone turned into werewolves pretty much as soon as the sun set. It was as you'd expect: their clothes ripped, they grew tails and thick fur. It was totally terrifying and gross at the same time. I really hate seeing them like that. I needed to get away, so Donny, Red and I shut ourselves into the Backstage offices and played a game of cards (Red won).

Then we all headed to bed—Donny and Red went into the offices that are now their bedrooms, and I set up camp in the Backstage kitchen. Before I fell asleep I took my potion out of the kitchen cupboard and left it by the window, in the light of the full moon. It was looking good, really good. Now that's been taken away from me . . .

The plan was simple: as soon as I woke up, the potion would be ready. I'd feed it to my family and they'd be cured.

But I should know by now that nothing ever, ever, ever, ever goes according to plan.

First thing this morning I yawned and opened

my eyes to see Professor Pickitt—aka Weaselly Scientist Supreme—standing by the kitchen sink. He was holding my potion jar up to the light and inspecting it closely.

"You really should lock your doors, you know," Professor Pickitt smirked as he started to tip the contents of my potion into the sink. "And you really shouldn't have made it so easy for me to ruin your silly little plans." He pointed to the label that said "Werewolf Cure" on the front of the jar.

That guy is as slippery as an eel in oil!

I threw off my sleeping bag and stood up. "GET OUT!" I shouted, my eyes nearly popping out of my head as I watched the last few drops of my potion wash down the sink. "Do you have ANY IDEA what you've just done?!"

I tried to keep my cool—but inside I was as far from cool as a snake in the sun. "Listen," I pleaded, "I know all you care about is making money. But all I care about is my family. And trust me—if it comes down to who cares more, I'll win."

"And how are you going to fight me all by yourself?" His eyes bulged and he looked like the kind of mad professor you read about in kids' books.

"He's not by himself," said a voice from behind me. "He's got us!"

Red.

A chair flew over my head and missed Professor Pickitt by a hair's breadth.

"You freak!" Professor Pickitt shouted at Red.

Suddenly all the cupboard doors in the kitchen flew open. Every can, packet, and box of food flew out of the cupboards toward Professor Pickitt's head. He ducked down but wasn't fast enough—a can of soup opened and splattered all over his head, followed by a drenching from

a carton of orange juice and then an entire bag of flour.

"Nice work," Donny whispered to Red.

Professor Pickitt looked as angry as an alligator. He stood up slowly, his eyes burning like radioactive flames. "Listen to me, you bunch of weirdos," he spat. "If you think you can stop me exposing the Feral werewolves with some silly potion, then you can think again! I will stop at nothing to get what I want. And I won't let you or anyone get in my way!"

Then he stormed past us, out of the kitchen and out of the Backstage offices.

My eyes met Donny's and I waited, hoping he'd make everything okay—like he always does. "My potion!" I wailed.

We both rushed over to the sink but the last drops had disappeared down the drain. "What am I going to do?" I whispered in horror.

"Make another one," Donny said simply—as if rustling up a werewolf cure was as easy as making a ham sandwich. "I hope you don't mind, but I took this from your school chemistry lab." He held up a small tube of mercury. I could have jumped up in the air and sung an opera—I've never been so happy in my life!

I stuttered with joy, "When did you . . . how did you . . . never mind, questions later."

"Now you're talking," Donny winked at me

and passed me the mercury. "Talk later, action now."

Without being told what to do I emptied the mercury into the empty potion jar. Maybe things weren't so bad after all?

"Red," Donny said, watching Pickitt slip away, "do me a favor and make sure Pickitt gets as far away from the zoo as possible."

"On it, boss," Red said, turning and running into the Backstage yard.

"You collect the frog eggs," Donny instructed me. "I'll go over to the reptile house and—"

He was cut short by a blood-curdling scream coming from outside.

I knew before I'd even left the kitchen why Red was screaming.

I could hear them howling. I could hear every word they were saying.

They'd escaped. They'd all escaped.

"He let them out!" Red shrieked at the top of

her lungs as she sprinted back in through the door to the Backstage offices. "I didn't get a chance to stop him. He was opening their cage door just as I stepped outside."

The three of us crammed around the nearest window. Sure enough, there were six werewolves prowling around the Backstage yard.

Er, heart attack! Werewolves on the loose!

"What are we gonna do?" I panicked. "We're cornered! My cure's been destroyed! We're sunk!" I stared at Red, who stared at Donny, who just stood there silently.

"Er, Earth to Donny!" I shouted at him. "This is serious! What are we gonna do?"

Concentration filled his eyes—I could see he was thinking mega-hard.

"Okay," Donny said calmly. "Here's what we do . . ."

Red and I listened carefully to Donny's plan. I was trying to stay calm. Although, for the record, staying calm when there are six escaped werewolves in the area is basically impossible.

"At least they're enclosed in the Backstage yard," I pointed out. "We'd be in serious trouble if they were loose in the zoo."

"Let's keep it that way," Red said, taking a step forward. She stared out of the window and I watched as every last piece of scrap metal in the yard flew toward the Backstage gate—barricading the werewolves in.

"I need to make another potion," I said hastily, looking down at the jar of mercury in my hands.

Donny pulled a silver dart from his back pocket. "Use this for starters."

"But what about everything else? I need werewolf fur, and all the other ingredients are in the zoo—how am I gonna get there with a pack of werewolves in the way?"

Red turned to me and gave me one of her wicked Red grins. "Getting to the zoo . . . now that's something I can help you with."

Suddenly I felt my feet leave the ground. "WHAT ARE YOU DOING?" I shrieked at Red as I rose into the air.

"Stay cool, kid," she smiled, concentrating on lifting me higher—soon my head was brushing the office ceiling. "You wanna get out of here . . . we're gonna have to fly you out!"

"Good call, Red." Donny nodded.

I heard the window behind me smash and looked back to see Dad resting his paws on the window frame and his head poking through the broken window.

"There you are, son," he growled. *"I'd like Sammy fingers for breakfast!"*

Before I had a chance to do anything, Red forced my body out of the window—my feet skimmed the top of Dad's head. Thinking quickly, I reached down and managed to pull out a chunk of Dad's fur as I zoomed past him. He leaped up and snapped his jaw at my hand but narrowly missed.

PHEW!

My body was flung through the air—hurtling at top speed. I didn't have a chance to think about how it felt to fly—it all happened so quickly. I zoomed over the werewolves, over the top of the barricaded Backstage gate, and landed on my butt with a THUMP in the main zoo.

I opened the jar I was holding and added Dad's fur to the mercury.

Out of the corner of my eye I saw a figure running away in the distance—Professor Pickitt!

Without pausing to think, I ran after him.

When I caught up with the professor he wasn't alone. Brenda, the journalist who turned up at our house yesterday, was standing next to him and writing something down.

"My dad told you to shove off!" I shouted at Brenda. "If you don't leave, I'll call the police!"

"You're a child!" she laughed back at me. "If I were you I'd run home and tuck myself into bed. Things are gonna get pretty busy around here today—every journalist in the country is on their way. By this evening the whole world will know what a freak show Feral Zoo actually is."

No one calls *my* zoo a freak show and gets away with it!

"Everything okay?" said a voice behind me. It was Seb.

"No," I replied. "The zoo's shut today," I told him. "Close the doors and don't let anyone in."

He frowned in confusion, "But, Sammy . . ."

"NO ONE!" I shouted. Seb looked frightened of me—my eyes must have been as wild as a werewolf's!

"No need to shout," Professor Pickitt said, smirking at me. "We can let ourselves out. But I'll be back, Sammy. And when I do come back, I'll be bringing every TV crew, every photographer, and anyone else I can find with me!"

Without another word, Professor Pickitt and Brenda walked away toward the zoo's exit.

"Sammy, what is going—" Seb started.

"I'll explain as we go," I interrupted. "Seb, I really need your help."

He could see the panic in my face. "Of course," he said.

As I led him to the reptile house I quickly told him the truth—I told him about Caliban, about my family, about Max, and about Donny and Red.

"You've been reading too many comics again," he laughed as I pulled an anaconda skin out of one of the snake tanks. Luckily there was one there.

"Fine, don't believe me," I said. I didn't have time to convince him. "But help me anyway, please."

Seb stared at me for a few long seconds without saying anything. Then he shrugged. "I've always liked you, Sammy. Whatever mess you've got yourself into—I'll help you get out of it."

So Seb and I got to work, running around the empty zoo and collecting everything I needed to create another potion: anaconda skin, frog eggs, and eagle feathers.

As soon as we were done we headed back to the reptile house and I combined the ingredients in the potion jar. "I don't have time to let it brew under the full moon again. I have to give it to them now."

"Sammy, you're starting to worry me," Seb

said with concern. "We should find your parents and . . ."

"Trust me," I said. "You really don't want to see my parents right now."

A loud howl shook the walls of the reptile house. The sound wasn't coming from all the way Backstage—it sounded much, much closer.

Seb didn't need to find my parents—they had found us!

"They've made it into the zoo!" I gasped in horror.

Then I heard Dad's voice—it was coming from outside the reptile house: *You think a few old chairs and garbage cans could keep us away!?*

Seb raced for the reptile-house door.

"NOOOOO!!!" I screamed, and lunged to stop him. But I wasn't fast enough.

Seb pulled open the door, but he didn't even have a chance to scream before Dad leaped on him, forced him to the ground, and bit into his neck.

No! Not Seb too!

My feet inched backward, my legs shaking like hummingbird wings.

Dad raised his head and his eyes locked on to mine. *"Seb's one of us now,"* he snarled. *"Don't fight it, Sammy. Join us."*

"I'd rather swim through a crocodile tank with raw steaks tied to my ankles!" I shouted defiantly.

Wolf-Dad did not like being stood up to! He tilted his head to the sky and let out a blood-curdling howl. Then he arched his back, ready to pounce. I looked around for a weapon or some way to defend myself, but there was nothing.

I psyched myself up.

I was ready to fight Dad with my bare fists, and if that didn't work . . .

. . . I was ready to turn into a werewolf . . .

. . . I was ready to die.

Then I heard Red's voice. "Sammy, duck!"

Without thinking, I dropped to the floor and watched as a huge silver water tank smacked Dad between the eyes, then thumped Seb (who was now half man/half werewolf) in the side of the head, before narrowly missing me.

Dad and Seb were both knocked unconscious.

"That won't keep them down for long," Red shouted at me from outside. "We need to run."

"Where're the other wolves?" I asked, jumping over Dad and Seb and joining her. "And where's Donny with his blowpipe when you need him?"

"He's trying to round up the other wolves—they're on the loose all over the place, trying to turn the zoo animals into werewolves!"

WHAT? A whole zoo full of werewolves! That was it, the battle was over. There was no way we could win. The situation was as bad as a chimp flying an airplane!

"We're doomed!" I screamed at Red.

"Werewolves . . . Pickitt. . . . It's all over, for sure!"

"NO!" Red shouted at me, placing her hands on my shoulders and shaking me. "Not for sure. Look at this." She grabbed hold of the skull necklace around her neck. "Donny gave me this. You know why?" I shook my head. "To remind me that death is the only certainty in life—we can't be sure of anything else. And if you accept that we're all gonna die anyway, then there's nothing to be afraid of. Okay, kid?"

"Okay." I nodded. I wasn't a fan of death talk, but if there was one thing I'd learned from Donny and Red, it was how to stay calm in a crisis. Red was right—until we were dead, there was still a chance we could get out of this.

But how?

My mind raced like a cheetah on roller skates . . . then an idea popped into my frazzled brain. "We have to corner the werewolves in one place," I said. "We can lure them together with bait."

"What bait?" she asked.

"Me," I said with a gulp.

Red nodded. "Okay, but first we've got to find Donny."

I was secretly hoping Red would have a better plan—but she didn't. It was decided: Sammy Feral = werewolf bait.

So we ran through the zoo, as fast as killer whales on an ocean raid. I kept the jar with my new potion close to my chest. At every corner I held my breath, hoping we wouldn't slam into a werewolf.

There was no sign of Donny, or any werewolves, anywhere.

We raced past the main gates to the zoo. A huge commotion was coming from outside. There were now hundreds of people, each one with a camera, waiting to get inside and catch a glimpse of the famous Feral werewolves.

One man was climbing the gate.

"What's going on?" Red asked, confused.

"It's Pickitt," I told her. "He's sent word to every journalist he knows to come here. He wants the world to know about werewolves— he wants to turn us into a freak show!"

"We can't let them get in!" Red said to me.

"How can I stop them?" I said back. "In case you hadn't noticed, we have a much larger problem to deal with—escaped werewolves!"

"You go and find Donny," Red instructed me. "Leave me here. I can handle this bunch. It'll take more than a few photographers to crack me."

"But, Red . . ." I argued.

"GO!!" she shouted.

I didn't need to be told twice—I needed to find Donny and the rest of the werewolves as quickly as possible.

I left Red by the front gate—she was shouting and using a broom handle to drive people away—and I carried on running through the deserted zoo.

As I turned the corner by the giraffe enclosure my heart skipped like a broken record.

Instead of giraffes inside the enclosure— there were werewolves. Only the werewolves were HUGE—giraffe-size huge! They weren't roaming around their cage, they were all lying still on the floor—it looked as if they'd been knocked out with something.

It didn't take a brain surgeon to work out what had happened.

"Sammy!" I heard Donny call.

I turned around and saw something metallic flying through the air toward my head. Holding the jar of potion in one hand, I caught the object with my free hand—it was a silver blowpipe. "It's my spare pipe," Donny shouted at me.

At that moment I saw a werewolf charge at me, out of nowhere. I instinctively raised the pipe to my lips and shot a dart. It worked. The wolf fell to the ground.

"Who's that?" I said, running over to the unconscious werewolf—it wasn't one I recognized.

"It used to be a hippo," I heard Donny call back at me.

That's when I saw Donny standing on the

other side of the giraffe enclosure—he was using his blowpipe like a machine gun, loading darts and blowing them at lightning speed.

Suddenly the sound of a hundred werewolf voices drowned out everything else around me.

The noise was deafening—it was enough to drive a sane person crazy.

The voices filled my head like a sinking ship filling up with water. I nearly dropped the potion jar as I reached up to cover my ears, trying to smother out the noise.

I felt as terrified as a tortoise on a busy highway.

Suddenly I lost track of everything around me—it was like I was drowning in a sea of syrup. I couldn't think about anything, all I could hear was the sound of hundreds of werewolves.

My head was pounding so badly I couldn't see what was going on. There were figures coming toward me—werewolves. I managed to raise the blowpipe to my mouth and blow into it as if the world was about to end.

The pain in my head got so bad I felt my knees give way. I fell to the ground, still clutching the jar and still firing darts. The pain got worse and worse and then suddenly everything went quiet.

I blacked out.

When I woke up, Donny was standing over me. We were in the reptile house. I quickly looked around and was relieved that the werewolves hadn't made it in here yet; the snakes still looked normal. Phew, at least Beelzebub was okay!

"Sammy, Sammy!" Donny shouted at me. "We need you. It's now or never!"

"What?" I asked, confused. The noise of werewolf voices still filled my head, but the walls of the reptile house muffled them enough for me to think. "What's going on?"

"There are too many werewolves. I brought you here so we can figure out what to do—I think your potion is the only hope."

"What about Red?" I asked.

"She's out there with the wolves," Donny replied. "There's nothing we can do."

I handed Donny the jar I'd been clutching. Frog eggs, mercury, and snake skin swilled around inside—it didn't look much like a werewolf cure; it looked like a stupid science experiment.

My heart sank in my chest. How was some stupid potion gonna save the day?

"It's all we have," Donny said gently, as if reading my mind.

As I took a deep breath I felt as if someone had flipped a switch inside my head—an instinct to survive had kicked in, big time.

"Okay," I said, taking another deep breath, "this is what we'll do . . ."

Donny listened carefully as I told him my plan. For once it was me giving the orders.

The plan was risky. There was a good chance we'd never make it—but we had no choice.

Donny opened a bag containing hundreds of small silver darts. "Good thing I brought these," he said.

I unscrewed the jar, tipped the darts in, and shook it around.

When every dart was coated in potion, we both stared at each other and nodded—it was time.

I stopped by the exit to the reptile house—I was ready to turn the handle, ready to face the wolves.

"Okay?" Donny smiled at me—there was a look of a madman about him, as if he couldn't wait to run headlong into a war zone.

"Let me at them!" I smiled back—feeling just as mad as Donny.

Donny kicked open the door and I made a run for it. I called the wolves in a language I knew only they'd understand: *"Follow me, follow me!"*

And I ran, the werewolves just behind me.

Were-tigers, were-lions, were-bears, were-crocodiles, were-hippos, were-zebras, and were-vultures chased after me as I bolted through the zoo. I led them past the parrot enclosures, around the monkey cages, and through the polar bear den, until we reached the fence to the giraffe enclosure.

It was the highest fence in the whole of Feral Zoo.

I began to climb.

My plan was working—the werewolves were following me. Every single were-creature in the zoo surrounded me as I reached the top of the fence.

I had just enough darts . . .

I shot down at the werewolves like a fighter-jet machine gun. A were-monkey climbed the fence and reached for my toes, but I shot it just in time. A were-hawk swooped down from the sky, its claws out, ready to kill—but I managed to land a dart in its chest.

When my hands were empty, that's when I noticed the silence.

The sound of werewolf howls, shouts, and snarls had disappeared. The ground was littered with bodies, and one by one the creatures were changing back into what they once were: lions, tigers, bears, hippos, crocodiles, monkeys, and humans. All I could hear was the beating of my own heart, and it was beating as fast as a Formula One racing car.

"It's worked," I heard Donny shout from down

below. For the first time since I'd met him his voice was filled with excitement. "Sammy, do you know what this means?"

"We've cured the Were Virus," I murmured, beginning to climb down the fence and looking at the sea of faces in front of me.

"Mom!" I screamed, charging toward the body of my half-human, half-werewolf mother, lying on the ground.

"Not now, Sammy," Donny instructed, as I crouched down over my mom and studied her closely. "We need to get this bunch moved before they're back to normal." He pointed toward the bodies of the animals lying around us.

Donny was right—I'd already fought off hundreds of werewolves; the last thing I wanted to do was start fighting a crocodile. We needed to get the animals back in their cages.

We worked together and it didn't take long. Humans Backstage, zoo animals in their rightful cages—simple. We started with the carnivores.

As we locked the last monkey into its cage I grabbed Donny's arm.

"Red," I said, concerned. "We left her."

We ran toward the zoo gates.

We were met by a scene of total chaos . . .

Seriously, journalists = more vicious than werewolves!

There were dozens of them. One woman was trying to climb over the gate. Another man was trying to squeeze himself through the narrow bars. Madness!

Red was working frantically to keep them out. Every time someone climbed the zoo gates, she batted them away with her broom. She was awesome—a proper emo angel. I was impressed.

"Butterfly nets!" she screamed when she saw us. Her black lips moved madly as she shouted,

"Grab nets, crocodile poles, brooms—anything you can get your hands on. This bunch is persistent!"

Donny grinned. "Let them in."

"Have you gone mad?" Red shouted back.

"Trust us, Red," I said with a huge smile. "There's nothing to see."

When she read the triumph on our faces she instantly knew what the plan was. She threw the broom she'd been using to the floor.

A young journalist nearly fell off the top of the gate as Red swung it open. Then a sea of reporters, photographers, and general nosy bystanders rushed into the zoo—each desperate to be the one to get the first glimpse of the Feral werewolves.

But there's no such thing as Feral werewolves. Not anymore.

All there was to see were a few battered cages and some trampled flower beds.

"One of the tigers escaped," I told the nearest journalist as a photographer took pictures. "It tore up the whole zoo. We spent hours trying to capture it again."

"That's why I worked so hard to keep you guys out," Red chipped in. "It would have been too dangerous to let the public in the zoo."

"Completely understood!" agreed the journalist and photographer together.

It didn't take long before the reporters got bored of taking pictures of sleeping animals. So they left. Pickitt was still shouting at them like a madman, begging them to stay and find the real werewolves.

But there are no real werewolves.

I'm still in shock.

I did it. I actually did it.

Sunday May 3rd

Sammy Feral = dude supreme!

It's official. My potion has cured the werewolves!! Even though it's still the full moon, everyone seems like they're back to normal. It's beyond awesome—who would have guessed I had it in me to create a werewolf cure? I wish I could tell my science teachers—no way would Mrs. Brown put me in detention again if she knew I was a potion-brewing genius!

Thanks to our world-class teamwork yesterday, the werewolves of Feral Zoo never made it into the national press, but the escaped tiger was in today's local newspaper:

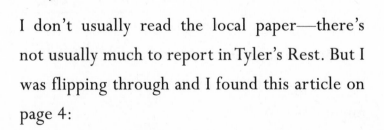

Feral Zoo Puts Visitors First

Award-winning Feral Zoo closed its doors to the paying public on account of an escaped tiger. According to reports, the tiger ran amok throughout the zoo, endangering the lives of those who work there. "It would have been too dangerous to have the public in the zoo," said one of the zoo's employees . . .

I don't usually read the local paper—there's not usually much to report in Tyler's Rest. But I was flipping through and I found this article on page 4:

Scientist Taken into Custody

World-renowned zoologist Professor Pickitt was arrested outside Feral Zoo yesterday. He was charged with disturbing the peace and wasting police time. Sources say that instead of being taken to jail the professor will be locked up in a secure hospital for the criminally insane. The professor allegedly believes that werewolves exist and have been running Feral Zoo, which given the first-class nature of the way the zoo is run (see page 1) is clearly untrue . . .

The ex-werewolves woke up around lunchtime today. As expected, they were seriously groggy. But groggy I can live with.

Mom, Dad, Grace, Natty, and Max all look human again, and Caliban looks like a normal puppy.

It's safe to say that I'm officially the most popular member of my family now that I've cured everyone of being a werewolf. I reckon I've got a good month of not cleaning my room, getting away with teasing Natty and Grace, and not having to do the dishes before people get fed up with me.

I just hope Mom and Dad are so pleased about the success of my potion that they don't think to ask me where I got the mercury . . .

"Donny's going to drive us home so we can get some sleep," Mom yawned at me. "We owe you our lives, Sammy. Thank you."

"I'm sorry I tore into you for making a potion," Grace said. "Who would have guessed my little brother could make a werewolf cure? Thank you, Sammy."

Don't get me wrong, I like being told how great I am, but I can't help but think that the potion could have been better. Sure, it worked, but there are a few werewolf traits it didn't cure:

* Excessive ear hair (Grace is NOT happy).
* Excellent sense of smell (Natty knew I hadn't changed my pants in three days just by catching a whiff as she passed me on the stairs).
* Fear of vegetables (I know, weird, huh? A healthy 5 on the scale, I'd say).
* Pack mentality (they all seem to know what the others are about to say).

Maybe if I make the potion again, and leave it to brew under the light of a full moon, it will be perfect. Maybe then I can offer it to Dr. Lycan and to any other werewolves.

I'm back at home now. Everyone's gone to bed and I'm in my room writing in my diary.

I'm not sure how I could feel happier. Now

everyone's cured, I feel like the whole world is turning just for me.

I guess there are some things that could make me happier. I wish that I could make things up with Mark, and I wish that now that everything's back to normal Donny and Red didn't have to leave . . .

Saturday May 9th

Sorry I haven't written in a few days—there's not been much to write about, really. In a weird way, life is starting to feel normal again. Don't get me wrong, there are still things that definitely register on the Feral Scale of Weirdness (like having ex-werewolves for sisters and gut worms living Backstage), but I think this is as normal as my life is ever going to get.

Mark's speaking to me again. I called him up and said sorry for being off the radar the last month. We've been hanging out every day since. Just like old times.

And Donny and Red have decided to stick around for a while.

I know, total awesomeness!

They're going to use Backstage as a base for their work. Donny still wants to learn more about my CSC and also keep an eye on my family—at least until after the next full moon.

"Your name's gonna go down in the cryptozoology history books," Donny told me this morning as I helped him feed some of Beelzebub's mice to the gut worm.

Donny being impressed by what I did makes me as happy as a dung beetle in a pile of steaming poo!

I'm hoping he lets me help out with other crypto-stuff in the future. I reckon my special talent will help me to become a world-class cryptozoologist one day! Imagine getting the chance to chat with a dragon, or a yeti?

But today I've just had gut worms and fire-breathing turtles to talk to.

Only a 5 on the Feral Scale of Weirdness.

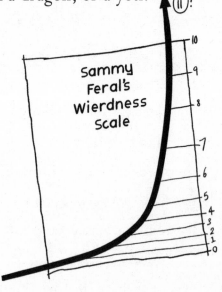

Sammy Feral's Wierdness Scale

Okay, to most people those animals would rank a maxed-out 10. But I know better; I know that things can only *ever* get weirder . . .